Edge

Drew A. Lennox

Introduction

Charlie

I close my eyes and take a deep breath. My heart is pounding, and I notice my hands have become shaky. My life is about to take a path I would have never imagined, not even in my wildest of dreams. I would lie if I said I wasn't nervous. I am so anxious but excited at the same time. To be honest, it's a feeling I want to remember for the rest of my life. It reminds me of the fight or flight response you get when faced with something difficult. I have either option at this point, and knowing the person I used to be, my first choice would be to flee. That's not the woman who is here today. Today I will fight, push myself to the edge, and break boundaries. He's prepared me for this, given me the tools to discover who I really am and who I want to be. I trust him, and I know he will keep me safe. Suddenly, I hear footsteps approaching. Opening my eyes, there he is, looking down at me, glaring directly into my soul, and I immediately feel calm. My eyes move up, looking at his hands. A small grin graces my lips when I see what he is holding.

"Shall we?" Xander asks.

"I'm ready," I reply.

Chapter 1

Charlie

What a day! I'm so glad it's finally Friday. This week has been one of the busiest I've had in a long time. I can't wait to get home, slip into some yoga pants, and enjoy a glass of wine on my balcony. This is probably the time I should introduce myself. My name is Charlotte Harris, but all of my friends know me as Charlie. I am twenty-eight years old and work as an elementary school teacher here in Baltimore. Originally, I'm from southern California but moved here about three years ago, following my boyfriend at the time. He had a great job offer, and it was either join him or break up. Unfortunately, both happened. We ended up breaking up six months after moving here. The first thing on my mind was going back home, but in just six short months, I had already built up a life and decided to stay. Best decision ever.

Even though I love this city, the dating scene sucks. It seems like everyone is just out for a fast hookup, no thank you. I'm not the type of woman that falls for those stupid games. Ok, I will admit, I did once, but lesson learned. Now I'm focusing on myself, fuck dating. I have a few terrific friends I've made over the years, and we usually meet up every other weekend for anything from concerts to shopping. Our group consists of Leah, Rachel, Brynn and myself...well, and the occasional boyfriend that comes along every once in a while. Currently, the four of us are single, and we had planned a girls' trip to Ocean City this weekend, but Rachel and Brynn ended up bailing. I suppose Leah and I could still go, but it's more fun when we are all together.

As soon as I walk through my door, the heels come off, along with the blouse and skirt. Walking into my bedroom, I grab some comfy clothes out of the dresser, put them on, and walk into the kitchen. It's only 4 pm, but I am starving. Opening the fridge, I look around and sigh. Damn, I really need to go to the grocery store. I've been avoiding it like the plague, stretching out what I have, but a trip there tomorrow is inevitable. Reaching for a container of leftover Chinese food, I pour the remnants into a bowl and stick it in the microwave. Once heated, I grab the bowl and take it to the dining table, along with the glass of wine I've been looking forward to all day. As I sit there, I browse the newspaper while eating. A few minutes later, I get a text from Leah, asking if I'd like to grab an early dinner tomorrow. Why not, I don't have any other plans anyway.

The next day I tackle the grocery store. I took my time and actually made a list, so this should be a breeze. After pulling up, I wonder why everyone, and their mother is here this morning. Grabbing a cart, I fight my way through the aisles, dodging people, and carts. A few minutes later, I hear someone say my name and turn around.

"Oh, Mrs. Landry, it's great to see you. Hey, Izzy," I say as I see one of my students with their mother.

"You too, Miss Harris. We just stopped in to pick up a few things for Monday's picnic. Izzy signed up to bring paper plates and cups," Izzy's mom informs me, and I'm glad I did run into her, I totally forgot.

"It should be a good time. Let's hope the weather plays along," I reply, and we chit chat for a few more minutes.

Once we say goodbye, I head down the beverage aisle and load my cart with water and juice packs. How did I let this slip my mind? That is definitely not like me. I'm usually on top of these things. Well, it's been a long week, I'll just blame it on that.

When I get home, I put the groceries away and grab a box of crackers, making my way to the dining table. Time to grade those papers! I teach second grade, and the kids just finished a math test. I have twenty-two kids in my class, and even though the math is simple, it's still a tedious task. Once the papers are all done and graded, I move to the couch and browse *Kids Art Projects* on my phone. I want to try something new, not the same old boring things.

Suddenly, a knock awakens me. Wow, did I seriously fall asleep? I haven't taken a nap in ages. Getting up, I walk toward the door and look through the peephole. Crap, it's Leah. Is it really that late? I open the door, and her eyes widen.

"Well, judging from what I am looking at, there is no way you are ready to go out," Leah teases as she steps inside.

"Yeah, sorry," I apologize. "I dozed off for a bit. I can be ready in ten minutes."

"No worries. We can order in too. What do you think?" Leah asks, and I couldn't agree more.

We decided to go with pizza, and about thirty minutes later it's delivered. Leah sets the box on the coffee table as I walk into the kitchen to get some plates and napkins.

"Oh my god, this looks amazing," Leah comments as she grabs a slice, putting it on her plate.

"I can't believe you've never eaten there before," I say, shaking my head. "Aren't you the pizza queen of Baltimore?"

"Ha-ha, very funny," she says, playfully shoving my shoulder. "You're right, though. I think I've tried every other pizza joint in this city."

We talk about the usual things while eating, work, guys, shopping, and more guys. Leah has been trying to fix me up with just about every single one of her guy friends, and even though I'm sure they are friendly, I just don't feel like dating right now. About fifteen minutes later, and after three slices of pizza, I sit back with the feeling of being unable to move. I should have stopped at two. Suddenly, the alarm on Leah's phone blares, making it sound like there is an ambulance in my living room.

"Holy hell Leah," I say as she tries to switch it off. "That could literally wake the dead."

"Sorry, but this is the only sound that gets me up in the morning."

"Why do you have your alarm set to go off at 5:45 pm anyway?" I ask curiously.

There's a takeover on LIFENET at 6 pm that I really want to attend. X. A. Taylor is going to be on then."

"Okay, you need to run all of that by me one more time. Who is X.A. Taylor, and what the hell is a takeover?" I ask, scrunching my forehead.

"You've never heard of a takeover? Are you serious?" Leah asks, and I shrug my shoulders. "Okay. A takeover is an online book event where authors showcase themselves and their books. It's a way to connect with them, and sometimes you can win free things as well."

"X.A. Taylor is the author, I assume?"

"Yep. I've been to a few of his takeovers, and he's very entertaining, a real hottie too," Leah smiles.

"What does he write?" I ask.

"Fantasy," she replies, and I raise one eyebrow. "Oh, not the boring kind. He keeps it interesting by combining several genres in the books. So sometimes you'll get some romance or suspense as well."

"Okay then," I say, picking up the pizza box and carrying it into the kitchen.

"Charlie, do you have your laptop around?"

"Yeah, it's under the TV-stand. Why?" I ask, and Leah gets up to retrieve the laptop.

"Here," she says, sitting down and logging into LIFENET. "I'll show you. It will be fun."

Joining her on the couch, she sets the laptop on the coffee table, and we wait for this author to appear. 6 pm on the dot, an introductory post seems along with a picture. Wow, he's definitely an eyecatcher, and that smile is amazing. The next post appears, asking where everyone is from and what time it is there. Immediately, Leah is typing away, and within seconds, I can't even keep track of all of the comments. I suppose this guy is really popular. About twenty minutes in, I'm hooked. This is such a cool event, and the author's answers are so witty and entertaining. He seems very down to earth, engaging with everyone. He and Leah go back in forth a little, and it's obvious they have interacted several times before. Once the hour is over, he says his goodbyes and posts several links, one to his books, the other to a LIFENET group, and one more to his website.

"So, what did you think?" Leah asks me.

"I liked it, really cool. I hope you win the e-book," I reply, and she smiles.

That night, I lie in bed, unable to get this man's smile out of my head. What the hell is wrong with me? He's a stranger, some author that I will never meet, especially since his genre isn't something that usually keeps my interest. Closing my eyes, I roll over onto my stomach, snuggle into my pillow, and find sleep within minutes.

After waking the next morning, I get up and go into the bathroom, turning on the shower. As I wait for the water to heat, my mind drifts to that intriguing smile that hasn't left my mind. There is something about him that pulls me in, fascinates me in a way. He came across as very friendly, open, yet mysterious in a way. Maybe I should send him a friend request. I roll my eyes and chuckle to myself. I don't read Fantasy, never have. What would I say? *Hey, I added you because I thought you were extremely attractive, and I think I may love your personality?* Nope!

After getting out of the shower, I dry my hair and walk into my bedroom to get dressed. Sitting on the couch, I grab my laptop and check my email. Shit, I have bills to pay. Reaching for my purse, I pull out my credit card and log onto the electric company's website to pay the bill. Next are the phone and water bill. I really need to set these on autopay; it would make my life a little easier. Placing my credit card on the table, I sit back with my laptop on my legs and log onto LIFENET. Looking through my updates, I comment on a few posts here and there. One of my friends back home just had a baby girl, and she is one of the most adorable babies I've ever seen. Interesting name too, Maeve, one you don't hear every day. After about fifteen minutes of browsing, X.A. Taylor is on my mind again. Fuck it. I'm just going to look at his profile. Typing his name in the search bar, his profile is at the top of the page. Clicking on his picture, I'm directed to his page and find myself lost within seconds. How can one person have over four thousand friends? That is insane! I may have about eighty on mine, but I can say I at least know every last one of them, personally. After a little back and forth, I decide to send a friend request. It's not like he will really notice me in the mass of friends he has, and I will at least have some cute pictures to look at every so often.

Xander

My alarm goes off, ripping me from my sleep. Holy shit,
why is it already morning? I feel like a zombie. Last night's
takeover was fun until these crazy women kept sending me
messages, and since I'm a nice guy, I made it a point to
answer them all politely. My posts were flooded with
comments as well, and before I knew it, it was 3 am. God
damn it, I need to stop being so kind to everyone.

Getting up, I walk into the kitchen and start the coffee
maker. Grabbing my laptop off the counter, I sit at the table
and decide to close out the giveaways this morning. After
logging in, I notice I have several new friend requests and
weed through them. One profile stands out, Charlotte
Harris. The name doesn't sound familiar, so I check her
profile, well at least what I can see of it since it seems to be
set to private. Maybe she's one of these crazy bitches that
will end up stalking me, I've had my share of them. Clicking
on her available pictures, I am immediately drawn to her
smile, just beautiful. When I get to the last one, I have a set
of gorgeous blue eyes staring back at me, wow. Maybe she's
a reader? Well, perhaps not, nothing book related on her
site as far as I can tell. Should I add her as a friend?

My coffee maker beeps, letting me know it's ready, and I get
up to grab a cup. This morning I'm going black for sure, still
need to wake up a bit. Sitting back down, I stare at
Charlotte's picture and wonder if she and I have met
somewhere. Maybe in a BDSM club? No, I would
remember her or at least recognize that stunning smile.
Getting down to business, I close out my contests from the
takeover, tagging the winners, and my mind drifts back to the
friend request. What the heck, I'll just add her, can't hurt. If

she ends up being a lunatic, then I'll just block her cute little ass. Chuckling to myself, I hit the accept button and write her a quick welcome message, something I do with everyone. Who knows if she will even respond, it's about 50/50 with people.

Damn, I almost forgot, I'm supposed to meet up with Shawn this afternoon to discuss his idea of building a dungeon in his house, and I also have to call my publisher about my current work in progress. Suddenly, I get a notification that I have a new message.

Chapter 2

Charlie

As soon as I click out of his page, I have a new message and assume it's from one of my friends back home. Clicking the message icon, my eyes widen when I see it's from the author I just sent the request to.

Hey Charlotte,

Thanks for the request, it's great to meet you. Just in case you don't know, I'm an author in the Fantasy genre. If you like to read, I'd love to send you one of my e-books to check out. Let me know!

-X-

So much for slipping into that friend list unnoticed. Well, now I have to reply, it would be rude for me to ignore the message. I'm sure it's something he sends to everyone anyway.

X,

Hey, it's great to meet you as well. I saw you at the takeover yesterday. My friend is one of your big fans. Sure, I'd love to read one of your books!

Charlie

That wasn't that hard. I'm sure he'll send the book, thank me for my interest and ask me to write a review once I read it... well... if I ever read it. Who knows, I may be pleasantly surprised. Another message notification.

Charlie,

I like your nickname. It's cute. I'm curious who is your friend? Also, I'll send you a copy of Stolen Dreams. It's my bestseller. I think you'll enjoy it.

-X-

Stolen Dreams. Well, the title does sound really interesting. Now I'm a little excited. What should I write back?

X,

Thank you so much. I look forward to reading it. My friend's name is Leah Holmes.

Charlie

Not even a minute later, another message.

Charlie,

Ha, yes, Leah! She's really cool and such a wonderful supporter. I consider her a friend of mine. Small world. So, I see you live in Baltimore as well, are you from there?

-X-

We continue messaging one another, and time just flies by. About two hours later, I tell him I have to log off and run some errands, and he says that he hopes to talk again soon. This is definitely not what I expected after sending the request. I really enjoyed talking to him, and it seemed as if the conversation just flowed, it was so easy.

I actually did have a few errands to run, and now I'm making sure I have everything together for tomorrow's event at school before I go to sleep. As I lay in bed, I pull up the

LIFENET chat app on my phone to see if I have any messages, and a smile comes over my face, it's a message from X.

Charlie,

Hello dear. Attached you will find the link to get your copy of Stolen Dreams. You don't have to create an account. It should just download on to whatever device you'd like to use. If you have any trouble, let me know, and I will be happy to help. I loved talking and getting to know you. Keep in touch. Sweet dreams!

www.bookworm.com/Stolendreams1423eckl

-X-

He loved talking to me, wow. Honestly, the feeling is definitely mutual. I usually do not talk to people online that I don't know, but I guess there is a first time for everything. Besides, we're just talking. It's not like I'm going to go meet the guy. I remember him mentioning that he lives in Ocean City, kind of ironic since that is where I was supposed to be this weekend. Clicking the attached link, I hit the download button and lay my phone on the nightstand. I don't read e-books and don't own a tablet, so I guess I will have to read on my phone. It's actually a good thing. I always have it with me so I can read it anytime.

The next day I wake up from my blaring alarm, and I hit the off button. Grabbing my phone, I check to make sure the book downloaded. Wow, what a gorgeous book cover! I wonder if he designed it himself? Clicking the messenger app on my screen, I search for X's name and start typing away.

X,

Thank you so much for the book. I've downloaded it and can't wait to start. By the way, did you design that cover? Hope you have a nice day today.

Charlie

Getting out of bed, I start my morning routine as usual. Pouring myself a cup of coffee, I still have a few minutes before I have to leave. Walking back into my bedroom, I grab my phone and see that I have a message.

Charlie,

Thanks! I hope you will like it. No, my publisher has a designer that does that for me. Good luck with your party today. I hope you have a good day as well.

-X-

Wow! He remembered that I have the school party today, how sweet of him. I start typing a reply, but after at least six different tries, I can't figure out what to say, so I just delete it and walk out of the door to go to work.

Thankfully, the weather plays along, and we can have our party outdoors in the courtyard. It was so great to see all of the kids with their parents. After the party, we walked to the classroom, and the kids proudly showed off their artwork on the walls. Seeing the joy in their little faces just melts me, and I can't wait for the day to have kids of my own... one day. When I get home in the afternoon, I start reading X's book. An hour later, I'm on chapter seven and don't want to put it down. He is an excellent writer, and I'm already hooked. As

I finish the last paragraph of the chapter, I see a message notification pop up on the screen.

Charlie,

Hope you had a great day, and everything went well with your event. I'm currently working on my next book and have writer's block. I suppose that's life, right?

-X-

Writing has never been my thing, but I'm sure this writer's block must be a challenge.

X,

I'm sorry to hear about the writer's block. I bet that can be very aggravating. The party was great, a nice change of pace. Oh, I started your book. Wow, I'm totally immersed in it. Just got to chapter eight. Did you have a good day today?

Charlie

I'm not even sure why I switched back to the book. I knew he would message me back within seconds.

Charlie,

I'm so happy to hear that you are enjoying the book. Chapter eight? Wow, you're fast. Maybe I should have you as one of my BETA readers. Yes, I did have a great day, really laid back, not much work today. That's the beauty of working from home. Any plans today?

-X-

What's a BETA reader? Well, I guess I'll have to ask.

X,

What's a BETA reader?

Charlie

I hope I don't sound like an idiot.

Charlie,

A BETA reader essentially is someone that pre-reads and critiques the writing. You know, see if it makes sense, points out spelling errors, and so on.

-X-

Ha, yeah, right.

X,

Pffft... I may be a teacher, but my strength lies in math. Well, if you would need one, I would try to help you out as much as I can. Back to your other question, I have no plans tonight. Just dinner and maybe watch TV. You seriously work from home? Must be nice.

Charlie

How do all these people find these work from home jobs? Maybe I should try my shot at becoming an author. Then again, perhaps not.

Charlie,

I'm not gonna lie. It's fantastic. I could just sit here in boxer shorts all day if I wanted to. I'll definitely keep you in mind as a BETA reader. An author can never have too many readers...and besides, you're growing on me.

-X-

Growing on him? Is that his way of giving a compliment? I guess it's cute, and my god, the visual of him in boxer shorts.

X,

OMG, are you seriously sitting there in boxer shorts right now?? Just kidding. Awe, I'm growing on you?

Charlie

Let's see if he picks up on my little flirtation.

Charlie,

No on the boxer shorts. Just wanted to see your reaction. Yes...you are growing on me. Oh, by the way, my name is Xander. I figure things are getting serious, and you should know, ha-ha.

Xander

He just shared his name with me, wow. I have to say I was so curious but didn't want to pry since I figured he wanted to keep it a secret. I totally chuckled to myself reading the *things are getting pretty serious* part. I love his sense of humor. I find myself laughing at our conversations and haven't smiled this much in a long time.

Xander

After re-reading our messages, one question does not leave my mind. Why do our conversations feel so familiar? The level of comfort we've reached in just a day is mind-boggling. In a way, it feels as if I've known her for a long time, yet we've never met. I could be wrong, making this into something it isn't, but what if I'm not? There is something about her. She's such a nice person. Should I get to know her better? What if I end up falling for this woman, and she won't accept my lifestyle? Why am I feeling this magnetic pull?

Speaking of my lifestyle, I practice **BDSM**. I am what you would consider a Dominant male or Dom. I've been living this way for the past twelve years and couldn't imagine any other way. Now here's Charlie, what if I tell her and she looks at me like I'm some sick individual? Wouldn't be so far-fetched, people do have their opinions about us, and most are afraid of the unknown.

What the fuck am I talking about? We've just met. Hell, I'll just keep messaging her and see how things develop. She may only become a fan, or we could just end up staying online friends, anything is possible. I can already hear my dominant nature growling like a lone wolf. I just need to be patient and take my time with her, really get to know her. My phone starts to ring, and I see it's Shawn. Chuckling to myself, I pick up.

Xander: Shawn, how's it going? Make up your mind yet?

Shawn: Fuck, no. I swear I had this vision in my head, but now I just can't see it happening.

Xander: It happens. Told you that you should have written things down.

Shawn: I know. I'm going to get started on that right away. You have a point. I just didn't think it would be that complicated.

Xander: Shawn, we're building a dungeon, not a master bathroom.

Shawn: True. Hey, so I called to see if you want to go to our favorite club this weekend. Max may be going too.

Xander: Um...yeah, sure, sounds good to me.

Shawn: Are you distracted?

Xander: You know me well.

Shawn: Let me guess, book, or chick.

Xander: Well, it's not a book.

Shawn: So, chick. All right, I want her name, age, measurements, place you met, years in the lifestyle, and most importantly, is she more of a brat or a sassy one?

Xander: Her name is Charlotte, Charlie, actually, and the rest I have yet to find out.

Shawn: Ok, you don't know where you've met her? Is she a ghost that appeared in your dream?

Xander: Fuck you, Shawn. No, I met her online. She attended one of my takeovers and then sent me a friend request. We've been talking since.

Shawn: Oh, so you don't even know if she's a sub?

Xander: No idea, my gut tells me no.

Shawn: Somehow, the pieces aren't fitting here. You're a Dom, why are you even talking to her? It doesn't make any sense.

Xander: There is something about her, I don't know. I've never been drawn to someone so quickly. There is this familiarity. I can't pinpoint it.

Shawn: Want my advice?

Xander: No.

Shawn: Well, you're going to get it regardless. I would be careful. It's the fucking internet. Don't get too invested before you know it's actually her you are talking to. I'll bet she will look nothing like her pictures.

Chapter 3

Charlie

Today is Friday, and spring break is starting next week. I'm really looking forward to having some time off even though I don't have any plans. I'm sitting at my desk while everyone is at lunch and decide to check my messages, and what do you know, I have one waiting for me from Xander. He and I have been in steady contact since meeting about two weeks ago. When he said he worked from home, I just assumed he was a full-time author. Nope, I was wrong. He's actually a software programmer for a large company based in Wilmington, Delaware. He said he started working from home about three years ago and bought a house on the beach in Ocean City. Must be nice. I would love to live at the beach and work from home too, but I suppose I didn't choose the right career field.

Charlie,

Hey beautiful. Hope those kids don't drive you too insane today. I've been working on a new book that may turn into a series. We will see. Hope we can chat later when you're home.

Xander

As usual, I have a smile on my face. I have about two minutes before my class returns, so I reply quickly.

Xander,

Well, my day is almost over, and I'm really looking forward to spring break next week. I'd love to hear about the new book. By the way, I'm about three-quarters finished with Stolen Dreams. I love it.

Charlie

Right as I place my phone into the drawer of my desk, the bell rings, and moments later, my students return from the lunchroom. Luckily, the afternoon goes by in a flash, and once everyone is gone, I get my things together and head to the conference room for a quick staff meeting. After sitting there for twenty minutes listening to useless information, we are finally released, and I'm the first out of the door. As I get into my car, my phone rings and it's Brynn, asking if I'm interested in meeting up for dinner and drinks tomorrow night. She also mentioned that the girls wanted to check out a new country bar that opened not too long ago. Usually, country music isn't my style, but guys in boots and cowboy hats are always nice to look at. When I get home, the shoes come off, and I take my phone out of my purse. Of course, Xander replied.

Charlie,

Spring break? Does that mean I get to take up more of your time next week? I'm not taking no for an answer, by the way.

Xander

Also...I'm glad you're enjoying the book!

His comment made me smirk. He's always direct, and that's what I love about him.

Xander,

Not taking no for an answer? I'll have to think about that one lol.

Charlie

Seconds later, my phone has another notification.

Charlie,

Think about it? You can't resist me, admit it. What's there to think about?

Xander

This one actually made me laugh out loud.

Xander,

You're right; you're irresistible. Sorry for my moment of insanity. How much did you write today?

Charlie

This is guaranteed to stop him in his tracks.

Charlie,

crawls under a rock Maybe 50 words? Don't kill me.

Xander

My eyes widen, this has to be a joke!

Xander,

50 words?! We've written more than 50 words in this conversation. What have you been doing all day? Well, besides work.

Charlie

On second thought, do I really want to know?

Charlie,

Wouldn't you like to know...?

Xander

There he goes being Mr. Mysterious again. I don't dig any deeper, though. When I did in the past, he would come up with some crazy replies that he had to have made up. We continue talking the rest of the night, nothing unusual about that. Most nights, I fall asleep with the phone in my hand. I used to get on Rachel's case, telling her she's glued to her phone and now look at me. Tonight, Xander wanted to find out a little more about me and was quite inquisitive. I told him I don't really have a so-called home. My dad was in the Navy, so we moved a lot. His last duty station was in Coronado, California, where my parents still live today. My dad is a pastor, and therefore I grew up in a religious household. Although I love my parents, I don't share their views and was happy actually to have the chance to branch out, moving away. My parents never coddled me, though. They have always been very involved in the church and their congregation, and to be honest, sometimes, it didn't leave much time for me. It would have been great to have siblings so things would have been a little less lonely, but my parents had a difficult time conceiving me, and my mom's pregnancy and my birth was complicated from what they've told me. I suppose I've been a pain in the ass from early on.

Xander

With spring break coming up, I'm already excited to have more of Charlie. I would love to surprise her with something. Maybe I can send her another book of mine? That's lame and could come across as selfish in a way. A moment later, I chuckle to myself, well there is one thing. I could always give her a good spanking session if she would like. I find myself smiling at just the thought, ok, the mental picture is really nice too. Or I could turn up the heat and give her a rough session. I'm definitely the man for that.

Many ideas run through my head, just none that would be appropriate. Except for the corset, that is a classy gift. Then again, she would be wondering why the hell I'm sending her a corset. Suppose I'd have to tell her what I'm into before I even think about that kind of gift. Damn, I would love to surprise her, but it seems I've lost my touch. How am I so bad at this? Well, note to self, tonight I will start on a new daily routine, reflecting on my day, trying to see what I can improve and what I've learned.

Getting back to my book, hoping to at least get another fifty words down, I stop about ten minutes later, thoughts of Charlie on my mind. I get up from my desk and go into my bedroom, returning to my office with a crop. Sitting in my chair, I play with the leather flap between my fingers. Moments later, I am lost in a daydream. I see her in front of me as I run the crop up and down her body, spanking the front of her thigh. Fuck! God damn it, I just knocked over a vase and sent it crashing to the ground. Great, it's definitely broken and worst of all, it's the vase my mom gave me sometime last year. Usually, it wouldn't be an issue, but it's one that's been in the family for years. How am I going to explain this the next time she visits? Sorry, mom, I got a little carried away and spanked the vase with my crop. That would go over well. I'm sure mom would be shocked if she had any idea of what I was into. I'll come up with some excuse because gluing the pieces is not an option...or is it? Hell, it's worth a shot. Picking up the pieces, I lay them on the desk and make a mental note to buy ceramics glue the next time I am out.

Tossing the crop on the chaise next to my desk, I get back to work, attempting to write a paragraph, but it's useless. Why is she always on my mind? How is it that we can chat all night, and neither of us runs out of things to say? This feeling is new to me. Usually, I am very disciplined. Hell, I've been practicing **BDSM** for a very long time, even helped others to get into the lifestyle, and now this woman is completely consuming me. What is it about her? To me, she is beautiful, innocent... like a lamb standing in front of a wolf. Well, Xander, great wolf you are. A wolf would lay low and hide, preparing to attack. I just stand out in the open, watching the lamb, completely mesmerized.

Sitting back in my chair, I run my fingers through my hair, what should I do? Tell her? I'm sure that would go over like a charm...*hey by the way, I'm into BDSM, and I have thoughts about you being my submissive.* Nope, not going to work. So, what can I do? I grab a pen and a piece of paper and write some notes for myself.

A: I will stay in contact with her in any way possible
B: I will wait for the right time to let her know
C: I will stay patient with her
D: I will not lose discipline

Walking into the kitchen, I attach the note onto my refrigerator with a magnet. Yes, looks good to me, I'll go with it. Deep down, I know that it will help me succeed. God didn't create the world in one day, so I can wait and be patient. Patience is the essence of this lifestyle. I do know I want more, way more. Messages won't be enough, in the long run, I'm dying to hear her voice. I'll make that my goal. I just need to make sure it won't be in a sexual way... well, maybe a little... but not too much. Next step after that? Meeting her!

Chapter 4

Charlie

I just made it to the restaurant and already see Rachel flagging me down. Surprisingly, I am the last to show even though I'm still early.

"Hey Charlie, I feel like I haven't seen you in forever!" Brynn says, hugging me.

"I know, it's been a few weeks. What have you all been up to?" I reply.

"Not much," Rachel begins. "A few dates here and there. Nothing worth talking about, though. Believe me."

"That bad, huh?" Leah chuckles, and Rachel shivers jokingly.

"Bad is definitely an understatement," Rachel says, rolling her eyes.

"Wow," I comment, and the four of us walk over to the hostess. Luckily, we don't have to wait and are seated immediately. This is one of our usual hangouts, a great atmosphere, and good food. After placing our orders, my phone buzzes on the table, and it's a message from Xander.

Charlie,

Getting ready to go out for the night! What are you up to?

Xander

I can't help but smile.

Xander,

I'm out with Leah and a few other friends of mine. Dinner, drinks and maybe some dancing. Where are you off to?

Charlie

My eyes stare at the message screen, another message, another smile.

Charlie,

Nice, I hope you have a great evening. Tell Leah I said hello. Just a club I frequent. Meeting a few friends there. You may hear from me here and there.

Xander

I feel myself beaming a little more than necessary.

Xander,

Message me anytime you'd like. I'm here XOXO

Charlie

Why the hell did I just put XOXO? He's going to think I'm out of my mind. Well, too late. Not like I can delete the message now.

"Earth to Charlie," Brynn says, waving her hand in front of my face.

"What?" I reply, putting my phone back on the table.

"And you tell me I'm glued to my phone?" Rachel butt's in. "We've said your name about four times until you finally acknowledged it. Must be one hell of a conversation."

"Sorry," I begin, just as my phone vibrates on the table again.

Glancing at the sender's name, I am eager to open it. I just sent him hugs and kisses out of nowhere. I need to know if he thinks I'm some crazy chick now. I take a quick, deep, unnoticed breath and swipe to the right.

Charlie,

Wow, I got some love ... I like it!

Xander

Well, I guess I worried for nothing, he received it very well, almost too well. I decide not to tell Leah hello from him. Me wearing this idiotic smile and telling her I'm talking to X will definitely bring some curiosity to the table. Don't even want to go there.

After dinner, we call a cab to take us to the country bar. Since we knew we would be drinking, neither of us drove to the restaurant. On the ride, Rachel decides to go into detail about one of her dates, and it takes everything in me not to burst out laughing. This poor girl, never a dull moment.

Once we pay our fare, we get out and head toward the double doors of the club. After paying the entrance fee, we walk through a set of saloon doors, and I'm surprised to see just how big this place is. A giant dancefloor on the right, which is packed with couples line-dancing. Straight ahead is a massive bar with what seems like endless amounts of alcohol. Looking over to the left, I see six pool tables along with darts and some high-top tables. I assumed it would be busy on a Saturday night, but this place is packed.

Heading in the direction of the bar, we have to wait a few minutes before the bartender gets to us. As we place our orders, a man in a plaid button-up walks up and tells the bartender to put the drinks on his tab. Immediately, Brynn strikes up a conversation with him, and within minutes they leave us and walk in the direction of the high-top tables. Well, that didn't take long. Usually, my money would have been on Rachel, but I guess after all of her disasters, the last thing she wants is to be bothered with another guy.

As the three of us stand near the dancefloor, watching everyone dance in sync with one another, I couldn't feel more out of place. I don't know the music nor the dance moves. I suppose I'll be the wallflower for tonight. As Leah, Rachel, and I are in the middle of a conversation, a man approaches us, asking me to dance.

"Oh, thank you so much," I begin, looking at this handsome stranger. "But I don't know any of the steps. I'll just make a fool of myself."

He chuckles, telling me he is one of the line-dance instructors here and that he's happy to teach me the basic steps. Hell, why not, it must be my lucky night. Leading me to a less crowded spot on the dance floor, he begins, showing me the moves, step by step. It's actually not as hard as it looked, and in no time, we are dancing together, having a great time. This guy, who by the way is named Corey, is really nice. We share a lot of laughs and, after talking for a while, have quite a few things in common. I could totally see myself dating a guy like this and secretly hope that he will ask for my number. Well, if he doesn't, I can ask for his, nothing wrong with a woman being proactive. After dancing, we make our way to the bar to Rachel and Leah. Brynn and Mr. *I'll Pay For Everyone's Drinks* join us, and we are becoming quite the little group.

"So, Corey," Rachel comments. "You are a pretty good teacher. You made Charlie look like a natural."

"She is a natural. To tell the truth, it isn't that hard. As long as you know the basic steps, the rest is easy to pick up."

After about twenty more minutes of conversation, I realize that Corey will never ask for my number. Just my luck, he is into men. It's typical that something like this happens to me, but on the bright side, I may have made a new friend. Feeling my phone buzz in my back pocket, I reach for it and smile.

Charlie,

Was just thinking of you. Hope you're having a great night.

Xander

Him saying that just made me beam.

Xander,

Hey! Yeah, we are having a good time. I just learned how to line dance. How is your evening shaping up?

Charlie

Immediately, another message.

Charlie,

My night is going okay. To be honest, I'm a little bored. You line-dancing? That I would have loved to see.

Xander

Xander

I decided to stay home tonight. I was looking forward to hanging out with Shawn and Max, but I'm not feeling a club tonight. Instead, I am at home, grilling myself a steak. As I stand at the grill, I wonder what I can expect of Charlie. Maybe I should start mentioning a few things about the lifestyle to her, gauge her reaction. I'm sure she wouldn't cut me off, we've gotten to know one another pretty well and enjoy talking. So why not share this crucial part of my life with her? I have nothing to lose, right? Well yeah, I may lose her. Damn it, what a struggle. I was dead set on only meeting a well-educated submissive. She would understand, and there would be no guessing or wondering on either part, but now there's Charlie, flipping my entire world upside down. I'm sure she's vanilla, I just have a feeling.

After dinner, I lie on the couch, with a flogger in my hand, Charlie's beautiful smile in my head, when a thought hits me. Who says she would even choose me or even want to meet me? I have never had so much self-doubt, what is she doing to me? I want her, all of her. Body, mind, soul...everything. She makes me smile with one simple hello, that has to mean something. I need to slow down. I'm getting way ahead of myself again. I'm a grown-ass man, but my thoughts make me seem more like an overly excited teenager. I need to be disciplined, and I will be disciplined.

Getting up, I place the flogger on the coffee table before something else falls victim to my daydreams. Luckily, I was able to fix the vase. Walking into my office, I sit at my desk to write. To my surprise, I finish two chapters, so I decide to jot down a few teaser ideas to submit to my publisher. For a moment I debate if I should message Charlie, I miss her but also don't want to intrude on her night out with friends. Instead, I surf the web, searching for new **BDSM** clubs, but I don't find any. Next, I look up some of my author friends to check out their latest releases, but my mind drifts again.

Chapter 5

Charlie

It is the first day of spring break, and it feels great to sleep in. Well, it's actually noon, but I was up until 4 am messaging with Xander. When it was midnight, I told him he should probably go to bed since he has to work in the morning, but he insisted he was fine. I don't know what it is about him, essentially, he is a stranger that I may never meet, but in a way, we are so familiar with one another. Conversations flow so smoothly, we don't run out of things to talk about, and I look forward to every message he sends. Since I basically skipped breakfast, I decide on a salad for lunch. After dousing my concoction in Italian dressing, I sit at the table and continue reading Xander's book. Right as I start the last chapter, I get a message notification.

Charlie,

How are you feeling today? Get enough sleep?

Xander

Very funny. I'm feeling playful, so let's see what I come up with.

Xander,

Sleep is overrated. Excuse me, but you are disturbing me right now, I am trying to finish a good book. Thanks.

Charlie

Can't wait for his reply.

Charlie,

Well, it better be my book!

Xander

Well then, let's play around some more.

Xander,

Maybe it is, maybe it isn't.

Charlie

This should be good.

Charlie,

So sassy. Maybe you deserve to be spanked.

Xander

Oh my God, I totally busted out laughing at this one.

Xander,

Ha-ha, I'd like to see you try.

Charlie

Luckily, I caught my breath long enough to send the message, him spanking me, sure.

Charlie,

Don't underestimate me, lol. I like a challenge.

Xander

Giggling to myself, I click out of the chat screen and go back to reading. About ten minutes later, I finish, and now I'm happy I explored something new. I absolutely loved the story and can't wait to read his others. I think he has another takeover sometime this week, and I want to make sure that I'm there to support him. Not that he needs it, his fan base is gigantic. I send Xander another message telling him I finished the book and just got done writing a review as well.

Looking at the time, I figure I should give my parents a call. I usually keep these calls to about once a week because there's only so much church talk I can take. They already aren't very happy that I'm not part of a congregation here. One day I will fess up and tell them that I just don't believe in it, but for now, I'll take the lecture.

After about twenty minutes, I'm surprised that the phone call went better than expected. Dad wasn't home, and mom was telling me about an upcoming trip they have planned to Colorado. She asked how things have been going here and if I've met anyone special yet. If it were up to her, I'd be married and on my third child by now.

As I lay my phone down on the table, it starts to ring, and when I see who it is, I immediately want to ignore it. It's a co-worker of mine, Jennifer Miller, one of the most annoying people I've ever come across in my entire life. She started working at the school about a year ago and, for some reason, thinks I am her best friend. Well, since I am a nice person, I suppose I will pick up.

Charlie: Hello, Jen. How are you?

Jennifer: Hey, Charlie, I'm ok. Listen, I'm sorry to be calling you, but our babysitter bailed on us last minute, and it's our anniversary. I was wondering if you happen to be free tonight?

Charlie: Umm, yeah, sure. What time would you like me to be there?

Jennifer: 7:30 pm. Mason should already be in bed so there won't be much to do. I would just rather have someone he knows to be here in case he wakes up.

Charlie: Of course, I totally understand. I'll be there.

Jennifer: I owe you.

Well, that's not so bad. I've babysat for them a few times, and I really do like Mason. From the sound of it, it seems as if I really won't have much to do. Maybe I should download another one of Xander's books.

Once I arrive at the Miller's residence, I tell them to have a good time, and after thanking me about a million times, they finally leave. Right now, I'm sitting on their sofa with Mason's baby monitor directly in front of me. He looks so peaceful lying in his bed, sleeping. Mason just turned two about a month ago, and I've never seen this child without a smile. Grabbing the remote to switch on the TV, my phone chimes on the table, and I grab it to see who it is.

Charlie,

Any plans tonight? Pulling another all-nighter with me? You know you want to. By the way. Thank you so much for the awesome review!

Xander

This is actually kind of perfect. I know talking to him will definitely make the time go by. Plus, I enjoy it. For a moment, I think back on our earlier conversation where he had me cracking up. Hopefully, he doesn't make me laugh too much right now. I'd hate to wake Mason.

Xander,

I am actually babysitting tonight. My co-worker's sitter canceled on her last minute. You're welcome, and I told you I loved the book. Already downloaded another.

Charlie

Which I doubt I will be getting to tonight.

Charlie,

Babysitting? So, you have the kids tearing up the house right now? Why didn't you tell me? I could have sent you the book for free.

Xander

I knew he would want to send me a free book if he knew I was interested in reading another one, but I'm happy to support him.

Xander,

It's only one kid, and he's in bed. Easy job for me. I wouldn't have accepted another free book, by the way!

Charlie

Grabbing the blanket off the top of the couch, I sit back and get comfortable. I can already tell we will be talking the rest of the night. How did I luck out in meeting such a great guy? All of our conversations put a smile on my face.

Charlie,

You really are a sweetheart. So, if you're not too busy, want to play a game?

Xander

Am I reading this, right? A game?

Xander,

Oh boy, why does this remind me of a horror movie? LOL

Charlie

It totally does, there was this movie where the character said, DO YOU WANT TO PLAY A GAME?

Charlie

LMAO! You crack me up. No just a question game to get to know things about each other. Are you up for it?

Xander

Questions? I love questions.

Xander,

Alright, let's do this.

Charlie

Now I'm definitely curious.

Charlie,

Damn, I like you! Ok, let's start with some easy ones. What's your favorite ice cream, furthest you've ever traveled, and the first thing you notice on the opposite sex? See, nothing crazy.

Xander

Hmm...favorite ice cream...this is a tough one. I'll go with the classic.

Xander,

Hmm...Chocolate, Sicily, and the first thing I notice are the lips. How about you?

Charlie

For a moment I reminisce on Sicily, I loved it there.

Charlie,

Mint Chocolate Chip, India, Eyes. By the way, yours are beautiful.

Xander

I can already feel myself blush. I think this is the first straight-up compliment he has ever given me.

Xander,

You are so sweet. Thank you so much! Have you ever been in love?

Charlie

After hitting send, I kind of feel like this is a stupid question. Of course, he's been in love.

Charlie,

No, I have not. Have you?

Xander

We continue this game for the next two hours. He's right. It's definitely a way to get to know things about one another. He's traveled to some fascinating places in the past, and I found out he is an only child like me. It's hard to believe that he's never been in love, he's thirty-five! How does that happen? I will say he kind of surprised me a little with questions like favorite sexual position and secret fantasies. To be honest, if it were anyone else, I probably wouldn't have answered and cut the conversation off right then and there. What is it about him that makes me want to share these things?

Xander

I was surprised to learn that she was babysitting tonight, well, like she said, it was a last-minute thing. I wonder if she loves babies, most women do. I'm thirty-five now and don't have any kids. Who knows, maybe I never will. For a moment, I wondered if babysitting was code for her maybe being on a date, but after she spent her entire evening with me, that definitely wasn't the case. If it were, I would feel sorry for the guy. Honestly, I have no claim on her anyway. She can see whoever she wants.

Sitting in my living room, I take a look around and can't believe how far I've come. Living right on the beach, beautiful house, nice car, work from home, successful author, great friends... and now I met Charlie as well. Life can't get any better, right? Though I cannot help but wonder what the purpose of our meeting is. I hope it's not another life lesson; I've had enough of that with Melany. That break-up was very messy, and I don't even like to think about it.

Looking at Charlie's profile picture, a thought crosses my mind. One day you will meet the real me, the Xander that will take you places you've never dreamt of and take you on unimaginable highs. Some things will be easy, and you may love them, but other things will test everything you've got inside of you. Of course, I want you to experience them, but one thing is for sure, once I have you, you are mine.

Chapter 6

Charlie

Opening my eyes, I turn to my left and grab my phone off the nightstand. Squinting to see the time, it looks like it's 10:30 am, and I'm still super tired from last night. Leah and I decided to go back to the country bar to hang out for the night. Unfortunately, all night turned into the early morning. It's kind of crazy. I was never someone who pulled all-nighters in my teens, and I suppose I'm making up for it now. Just like every morning, I open the messenger screen to text Xander. I know he's wide awake and has probably written half a book by now. Typing the message, I think I hit send but instead hit the call button. Immediately I drop my phone in a panic. As I try to pick it up to end the call, I hear a voice on the other end. A sexy one, if I may add.

Xander: Charlie! What a surprise.

Closing my eyes and mumbling the word FUCK under my breath, I inhale deeply and put the phone to my ear.

Charlie: Hey! Yeah, I figured I'd just give you a quick call to say hello.

Xander: You accidentally hit the call button, didn't you?

Charlie: Yup! How did you know?

Xander: Had a feeling. Anyway, since I have you on the phone, let me run something by you, I just wrote.

Running something by me, he just wrote turned into a three-hour conversation. Now I am delighted I hit that call button. It was so comfortable, so familiar, and his voice... oh my god! I could listen to him talk all day. Usually, I am very quiet when it comes to phone calls since we live in a world of texting, but there was not one awkward moment with him. I seriously felt as if I've known him for years. Oh, and the laughs we shared, amazing.

Over the course of the next few days, Xander and I switched from messaging to phone calls. Well, we still message each other during the day, but calling is just much more personal. We talk about everything from what we are making for dinner to crazy moments in our teenage years, well, more his teenage years. So many laughs. I told him that I will hold him responsible for the laugh lines he is giving me, and he better be prepared to pay to have it reversed. Of course, I'm just joking.

Tonight, Leah, Rachel, and I are invited to Brynn's place for dinner. Well, Mr. *I will pay for your drinks*, aka Ryan will be there as well. Yep, you guessed right. He's the new man in her life. Actually, none of us knew that they were dating; she was sneaky and kept that from us.

Walking up to her door, I ring the bell, and to my surprise, Ryan answers.

"Hi," he begins. "Charlie, right?"

"That's me," I reply as he steps aside, asking me in. "It's great to see you again, Ryan."

"You too, Brynn is in the kitchen finishing up dinner. Can I take your coat?"

"Oh, thanks," I say, handing it to him before heading toward the kitchen.

"Hey, girl! You're the first to arrive, not really surprised though," Brynn comments as I notice the hurricane that has swept through her kitchen.

"Do you need any help?" I ask.

"I'm good," she replies as the doorbell rings.

Moments later, we are joined by Rachel, Leah, and Ryan, and I will admit, it's different having a guy here, especially one we don't really know. It's funny to see *new* couples interact though, lots of cute little uncertain smiles.

I will say Brynn outdid herself with dinner tonight, so delicious. The five of us are sitting in the living room, talking, and I think I really like Ryan. He shares that he has a seven-year-old son that goes to the same school I teach at. Who knows, maybe he will be in my class next year. Since I told Xander I would be out this evening, we've resorted back to messaging. I haven't told anyone about him, and honestly, why would I? He's just a friend. Though I think Leah has suspicions since she and I have been meeting at his takeovers and my interactions with him are very friendly. I'm actually surprised she hasn't made any comments, one of her favorite pastimes is to tease me.

"All right, guys!" Rachel says, stretching out her arms. "I'm going to head out.

"Yeah, me too!" I say, getting up from the couch. "I have to be up early tomorrow. Ryan, it was great seeing you again."

Once I get to my apartment, it doesn't take long until I crash. I've never been so happy to see my bed. Thankfully, tomorrow is Friday, and I already told everyone I'm staying home this weekend.

Upon arriving at work today, I had a memo in my box that says we will be having a staff meeting after school today. I'm sure it has to do with summer break, even though it's still about two months away. Currently, I'm sitting in class and just handed out a quiz. Sitting back in my chair, I can feel my phone buzz in my desk drawer, and I open it slightly just to see who it is. Looking down at the screen, I notice it's a message from Xander, and I smile immediately. Even though I want to see what it says, I make sure not to use my phone during class. About ten minutes later, my timer goes off, and I ask the students to lay down their pencils. After collecting the quizzes and placing them into my bag, I ask what they have planned for the upcoming weekend. I love second graders. They are so excited all the time. I will say this has been one of the best classes I've ever had, and I will miss them when they move on to third.

As I figured, the meeting was about summer, and I'm surprised to learn that I will have a new teacher shadow me for a few weeks when we start back up in August. When I get to my car, I remember the message I got earlier and take out my phone to see what it says.

Charlie,

I was just thinking of you. Hope you're having a good day! Call me later.

Xander

Sitting back, I let out a sigh. I've been thinking of him as well. Actually, it seems as if he never leaves my mind. The more we talk, the closer we get.

After eating dinner, I change clothes and lie on the couch to call Xander.

Xander: Charlie! I missed you.

Charlie: Hey. You sound excited!

Xander: Well, I'm just happy to talk to you. How was your day?

Charlie: It was alright. I'm happy it's Friday. How was yours?

Xander: Great, actually. I got a call from my publisher today saying they will be picking up my new book as well.

Charlie: Oh my god, Xander, that is fantastic news. Congratulations.

Xander: There's more.

Charlie: Oh yeah? Let's hear it.

Xander: Well, I have to meet with them in June, and they are in Baltimore. I was wondering what you think about maybe getting together for coffee?

Charlie: Yes!

Xander: Wow, that was quick.

Charlie: Sorry, just got a little excited.

Xander: Well, I am excited to meet you. I'll be there on June 7th. The meeting is at 3 pm, and I thought we could meet later that evening. It's still a bit away, and we can figure out the details later.

Another three-hour phone call. Well, at least I wasn't sitting on my ass the entire time. I got all of my cleaning done and paid my bills. Oh my god, I can't believe we are going to get to meet each other! Excited isn't even the word for it. I hope we click as well in person as we do online.

Xander

Damn, I love her voice; she sounds like an angel, so beautiful. I really could just sit there, sipping my coffee, and listen to her for hours on end. Fuck my life, she is amazing. I know it may sound crazy, but if someone would ask how I would picture the woman of my dreams, I would say it was Charlie. I know what you're thinking, how can she be? I don't even know if she will be compatible with my lifestyle, but I have a feeling. Deep down, I know she could ask me anything, and I would answer it, no matter how embarrassing it is. Actually, it's a wonderful beginning to a close bond, a huge part of the foundation of the lifestyle. Talking and establishing a deep connection is never a bad thing. In time I will tell her all about the bond shared between a submissive and their Dom, but for now, I may just try to secretly build it.

I can't wait to meet her, and from the sound of it, she feels the same. Knowing me, I will study her every move, her body language, what she does when she gets nervous, I'm very observant. I just have to make sure to be less obvious about it. I don't literally want to look like a wolf, at least, not yet.

Chapter 7

Charlie

We are going to meet! I can't wait! What in the hell am I going to wear? I really need to go shopping. Ok, Charlie, slow down, you still have time. A part of me wonders why I am putting in so much effort. He's just a friend. Well, a friend I talk to for hours on end, every day. Sometimes our conversations get very flirtatious, but he didn't say this was a date. Maybe I'm just overthinking. I need to take a deep breath and stop second-guessing.

"Charlie, your turn," Leah yells out, and I'm shaken from my daydream.

Lining up the cue stick, I take my shot and miss. Damn! Well, I'm not surprised, I suck at pool. To be quite honest, Leah isn't a star player either, so the game is pretty fair.

"So, I have a date this weekend," Leah begins. "It's a guy from work."

"Oh yeah? Anyone, I know?" I ask.

"Actually, yeah, remember David? He came out with us a few times last year."

"David?" I say, thinking and bouncing my cue stick on the ground. "Oh, motorcycle David?"

"That's the one," she replies.

"Wow, really? I thought you hated him." I ask, recalling a lengthy conversation she and I once had about him.

"Well, he kind of grew on me," she admits. "He's actually very sweet."

"Well, I'm happy for you, where are you going?"

"Dinner at Donatello's," Leah replies.

"Fancy! Is he picking you up on his bike?" I chuckle.

"Charlie, you're an ass," she jokes, shoving my shoulder. "He also owns a car, a very nice one at that."

After we finish the game, which by the way I won, Leah tries to play matchmaker again, listing all kinds of eligible bachelors she knows. After rattling off god knows how many names and what they do for a living I decide to tell her I have a date in a few weeks. The look on her face is priceless and full of curiosity.

"So, that's it. You're not giving me more information?" Leah begins.

"What's there to say, it's a guy I met a few months back, and we are meeting for coffee," I say.

"Umm...name, age, location, profession, is he hot...I could go on," Leah presses.

"Well, I'm not telling you his name or location; you will end up stalking him. He works in the computer world, thirty-five and yes, he's a very good-looking man," I say, thinking this won't give anything away.

"Did you meet him online?"

"Yes," I answer, and she makes a face. "What?"

"Well, do you know if it's really him?"

"Yeah, why?" I ask, wondering what she's getting at.

"Well, I just want to make sure. There are so many people out there pretending to be someone they are not."

"You're right. Well, we've talked on the phone a lot," I say.

"Have you video chatted with him?"

"No, I haven't," I say. "Do you think I should?"

"I would bring it up. If he says no, then I'd be suspicious. It's happened to me before, and after that, the profile mysteriously disappeared," she explains, and I remember her telling me about a story like that before.

When I get home that evening, thoughts run through my head. What if Xander really isn't who he says he is? He only has a few pictures online. I would be devastated, we've become so close, and I've told him things I've never told anyone else. A few minutes later, I get a message from Xander.

Charlie

Hey beautiful. Hope you had a fun time with Leah. I've had a rough day, so I'm calling it a night. Sweet dreams, love.

Xander

Probably not the time to bring it up.

Xander,

I'm sorry to hear. Sleep well and sweet dreams to you too! xoxo

Charlie

The next day I am up earlier than usual, so I throw a few ingredients into a crockpot to simmer while I'm at work. I also have enough time to stop by a coffee shop in the area. I've never been here before, and as I wait for my coffee; I look around and think this may be the perfect place to meet Xander. Comfortable sofa chairs tucked away in corners, leather couches, and great background music. I will definitely keep this place in mind.

Sitting in the teacher's lounge at lunch, Jen sits next to me and starts talking about Mason. I welcome the distraction; my mind is still running 100 miles per hour after my conversation with Leah yesterday. Maybe her idea with the video chat isn't so bad. I'm not really a fan of it, but I want to make sure it's him.

When I get home that afternoon, I'm met with a delicious smell coming from my kitchen. What a great idea this was, no cooking for me tonight and leftovers for the next two days.

Later that evening my phone rings and I know exactly who it is.

Charlie: Hey Xander.

Xander: Hello, gorgeous. How was your day?

Charlie: It was good. I got up early and went to a coffee shop nearby. I liked the atmosphere and figured it would be an excellent place to meet.

Xander: What is it called?

Charlie: Diablo Coffee.

Xander: Cool, I'll look it up. Everything ok?

Charlie: Yeah, why?

Xander: You just don't sound as chipper as you usually do.

Charlie: Can I ask you a question?

Xander: Of course, anything. You know that.

Charlie: How would you feel about video chatting?

Xander: Video chatting? Do you want to see me?

Charlie: Yes.

Xander: All right. Let me call you back.

Charlie: Wai-

Before I can continue my sentence, he is gone, and now my phone is ringing, and the screen displays *Xander wants to video chat with you.* Great, I look like shit! Taking a breath, I hit the accept button, and there he is, staring back at me, waving. All of my fears were unwarranted; it's him. Even though we've been talking to one another for months, I find myself a little shy and keep stumbling over my words. About ten minutes later, things return back to the way they are when we talk on the phone, making it comfortable. His eyes, wow, I could get lost in them. They are a gorgeous shade of hazel, and his stare is so intense, almost as if he is studying me. One look into those eyes, and I can already feel myself get weak.

Xander

Did we really just video chat? I'm honestly shocked that she brought it up in the first place. From the tone of her voice, I knew precisely that she wasn't ready to do it right then and there, but I wasn't giving her an option...why not display my dominant nature now. Worked out pretty nicely. Seeing her was amazing. There's something about seeing a person move, laugh, blush, and even though it's not the same as standing in front of someone, it's more personal than just a voice call. I loved how she stole a glance at her own picture every once in a while, fixing her hair and removing a make-up smudge under her eye. I'm sure she thought she wasn't put together enough, but for me, she was perfect.

Going into the kitchen, I make myself a sandwich and walk out on my deck. Looking at the ocean, her eyes don't leave my mind. So blue, almost like the water. She has this innocence about her that draws me in, makes me want to discover all of her, conquer her. Standing against the railing, I reflect on my day. I wrote another chapter, came up with an idea for a new book, talked to my mom, video chatted with Charlie. Overall a wonderful day. We stepped up our form of communication, and it felt comfortable, that has to mean something. We can talk about anything from childhood memories to sexual experiences. I will admit, I am keeping mine PG-rated for now. We have plenty of time to get into all of that. Even though I loved seeing her, and I was the one that pushed for video chat after she mentioned it, I wonder if we need to make sure we don't rush things. I just want to make sure that we don't turn into something that is fast and furious, lasting only two or three months before it all falls apart. Once I'm invested, I won't want to let her go. Hell, I'm already invested.

Chapter 8

Charlie

Why is it that when you are waiting for something, time doesn't seem to go by? Well, okay, it's the end of May, I'm exaggerating just a bit. Damn, I want to see him, in person that is. We've alternated between calls and video chats in the last few weeks, and I feel as if it's brought us a little closer. With that being said, I love seeing him, but he always hits that damn video call button at the worst moments. When he called the other day, I had just put a hydrating mask on my face, and my hair was in a messy bun on top of my head. I suppose I didn't have to pick up, but I have this weakness for him. The good thing is that I am willing to him see me when I look like shit, another thing that speaks volumes. I honestly don't remember if my last boyfriend ever saw me without makeup, kind of sad in a way. Well, that's the past, who cares?

I love that I can be me around him and don't have to put on some kind of façade. Sitting in class, I wonder how our first date will go. What if we meet and there is zero chemistry, which I doubt, but it's possible. Here we go again, no one said this was a date, we're just friends, very good friends, maybe even best friends. In any case, I need to go to the mall after work to look for something cute to wear to this *date-but-not-really-a-date.*

Looking around the classroom, I see all of the kids, quietly reading their books. To be young again, no worries, no second-guessing. Their worries are what flavor ice cream they want or what toy they want to play with. Then again, I'm happy I'm not that age anymore. I remember a lot of lonely times in the church breakroom while my parents engaged with the people attending service. Sometimes the occasional kid would join me, and we would play, but I was quite shy and quiet growing up. Maybe it's because I wasn't exposed to much. I may have traveled to many different places but didn't really experience them until I hit my teens. In college, I wasn't any different; the shy girl buried in her textbooks. College was hard for me, my best friend was supposed to be with me, and we were supposed to go through this experience together. Her name was Leslie, and we met when we were thirteen years old at, you guessed it, a church function. Leslie didn't come from a religious background but wanted to explore the whole church thing for herself. Once in a while, her parents came along with her as well. I always loved them, and their place became my second home. I remember spending many dinners with them. Leslie was one of six kids, and I just loved being a part of a big family. Then we turned seventeen and went out to a party, that's when everything changed.

God, I don't want to think about that right now. A moment later, the bell rings, announcing the end of the school day. I tell my students to have a great day and not to forget to give the permission slips to their parents for our upcoming field trip.

Once I get everything together, I head to my car and drive in the direction of the mall. I love to shop, but not when I'm under pressure. Let's hope I find something I like. After going through four stores with no success, I stop by the food court and have some sushi to refuel. Pulling out my phone while eating, I know, bad habit, I send Xander a message, telling him I'm at the mall shopping. Like always, I hear back right away, and his response makes me choke on the tuna roll; I just put into my mouth.

Charlie,

Let me guess, shopping for something to wear for when we meet.

Xander

How in the hell did he know that? I never mentioned anything to him.

Xander,

Whoa, how did you know?

Charlie

Let's see what he replies.

Charlie,

It's just a feeling I had. So how is the search going?

Xander

A feeling, huh?

Xander,

Not so good. I have about three more stores to hit up before I say fuck it.

Charlie

Ok, Charlie, you don't have to tell him everything.

Charlie,

I know you will find something you like. Take your time and enjoy. Just in case you don't find anything you like, remember, naked is always an option as well, my dear.

Xander

My eyes widen.

Xander,

Oh, I'm sure you'd like that. Not happening, buddy.

Charlie

I may have chuckled just a little on the loud side. I got the attention of the couple seated at the table next to me.

Charlie,

Actually, I wouldn't want you naked. I like it when something is left to the imagination, much sexier.

Xander

Oh, that's right, he's one of those guys... that is if he's not bullshitting me.

Xander,

Noted. All right. You just made it easy. I'll show up in a burka. Thanks!

Charlie

Clever Charlie!

Charlie,

Sassy girl. You're lucky I'm not there, otherwise...

Xander

And he stops his sentence, classic Xander.

Xander,

Otherwise what? I hope you're not one of those guys that talks the talk but can't walk the walk.

Charlie

Well...I already sent it. Now I feel stupid.

Charlie,

You have no idea. I will always walk the walk... just wait and find out for yourself.

Xander

I decide to send him an eye-roll emoji before throwing away my trash and continue my search for the perfect outfit.

Xander

I must admit, I love that sassiness. Maybe more so because of all the things I imagine to rectify that behavior. Running my hand over the dining room table, I would love nothing more than to have her bent over, hands on the table, anticipating the paddle. That image alone does things to my mind, making my body react. Damn, we've never even met in person, how does she do this to me? Well, not too much longer, patience Xander.

I'm on my way to meet Shawn for a quick bite to eat at one of our favorite places. It's a small hole in the wall that has been around for years and serves some of the best appetizers I've ever had. Once I pull into the parking lot, my phone buzzes in my pocket, and I assume it's Shawn telling me he is going to be late. Reaching for it, I smile, it's a message from Charlie.

Xander,

Good news. I won't have to wear that Burka. I'm heading home to grade some papers.

Charlie

Damn, I was just getting used to the idea of seeing her all covered up...not!

Charlie,

See, I told you. I'm just pulling up to meet one of my buddies for dinner. I'll message you once I'm home.

Xander

"Hey Xander," Shawn says, getting out of his car, next to mine.

"What's up man," I reply before rolling up my window and getting out of the car.

"Not much, got some ideas for the dungeon," he smirks.

"I hope you didn't choose the cliché colors," I respond as we walk toward the restaurant.

"You mean red and black? They may be cliché but classy as well."

"Yeah," I begin. "I guess you're right. I'd go a different route, though."

"Oh yeah? What would your choice be?" Shawn asks as we walk through the door.

"A dark blue with some black and possibly some white," I reply, imagining it in my head.

"That's...different. I have a hard time picturing it for some reason, what the fuck would be white?"

"The furniture," I reply.

"I'm not convinced," Shawn chuckles.

"Well, the good thing is you don't have to be; it's my dungeon."

Chapter 9

Charlie

Charlie,

Hey! Just got to the coffee shop. I will wait for you outside. See you soon!

Xander

Great! He's already there. Scolding myself for taking so long putting on my make-up. I get into my car and hurry to the coffee shop. I am so happy I chose this place, it's close to my apartment, so I at least have that going for me. Luckily, I find a spot right away and rush to the front of the building. Turning the corner, I spot him, glancing down at his phone. He is even more handsome in person, and I can already feel myself shaking from nerves.

"Charlie?" he says, flashing that million-dollar smile.

"Hey Xander," I reply, walking toward him. "I'm sorry I'm a little late."

"No worries," he replies, pulling me in for a hug. "Wow, I'm so glad to finally meet you. Even though it feels like I already know you."

"I know what you mean," I say, still lost in his embrace. "It feels the same for me."

Standing back, we look at each other for a moment, and I can feel my cheeks burn. God, why am I so nervous. Here he is, standing there all calm and collected. Well then again, he's always come across this way, why did I expect anything less?

After chatting for a few more minutes, we decide to head inside, and he opens the door for me. Standing at the counter, I go with my usual café au lait, and he orders a cappuccino. As I reach into my purse to grab my credit card, Xander gives me a slight smirk.

"Not happening," he comments. "I invited you."

"So, had I invited you, I could pay?" I ask with a grin.

"Nope," he counters, and for some reason, I had a feeling he would say that.

Once our drinks are ready, we walk to the back right corner of the shop and make ourselves comfortable in two large plush chairs, separated by a small side table. After placing our drinks on it, our eyes meet, and immediately I chuckle.

"Do you feel weird?" I ask, and he cocks his head to the side.

"Weird?"

"Well, I guess I meant strange. Is it strange sitting across from someone that you know but then again kind of don't?" I say, feeling like an idiot for even saying it, damn nerves.

"Not strange at all, more familiar," he pauses to take a sip, "and very happy. Do you feel strange?"

"Maybe strange was the wrong word. I think I meant nervous, actually. I know just about everything about you, yet this is new."

"I can promise you've yet to uncover everything about me," he replies, winking. "Please don't be nervous. I'm just me."

"Now I'm intrigued," I counter. Him being mysterious makes him even sexier.

"Well, if you stick around, you may find out more," he chuckles, and I roll my eyes.

"As if I'm going anywhere. You'll have to try harder than that to get rid of me. We're kind of like best friends," I say, and he raises an eyebrow.

"Best friends?" he counters, leaving me puzzled.

"Well...umm," I mumble, and before I can utter another word, his hand grabs mine, making my heart pound.

"I see more for us to be quite honest," he says, looking me straight in the eye.

"You do?" I reply, cheering silently inside.

"Yes. I find myself thinking of you more than I'd like to admit. I don't know what it is, but I feel like we connected on a deeper level."

"I feel the same," I reply, still holding his hand.

He smiles at me, one of the most beautiful, honest smiles I've ever seen in my entire life. We continue our conversation, and all of the jitters disappear. It's just like our phone calls, comfortable. No awkward moments, no pauses, just flowing conversation.

We finished our coffee's over an hour ago but still find ourselves lost in conversation, lost in each other. I've never met anyone I mesh with so well. Our interests are quite similar. We love the same music, have the same hopes and dreams. How did I get so lucky?

"All right, everyone, ten minutes until closing time," the barista announces, and I can't believe we've been sitting here for over two hours. Then again, it doesn't actually surprise me.

"Well, I suppose they are kicking us out," Xander comments and I smile.

"Seems that way," I reply, getting up from my chair.

Xander grabs both of our empty cups and throws them into the wastebasket before taking my hand and leading me out of the shop.

"Where did you park?" he asks curiously.

"Around back," I reply. "How about you?"

"Across the street," he smiles. "I will walk you to your car."

God, I wish this walk were longer, but in no time, we are standing at my car, and I hit the unlock button.

"Thank you so much for tonight," I begin. "I am so happy that we finally met."

For a moment, he just smiles, looking into my eyes. I can feel my pulse quicken in anticipation that he may go for a kiss. The look in his eye is a dead giveaway, yet he's holding back.

"Me too," he replies, pulling me in for a hug. "Silly question, but would you like to go out again?"

"Definitely," I say, a little too quickly, making him laugh.

"I know it's tough with the distance, but let's see if we can set something up. I'll call you as soon as I get back to the hotel."

"Thank you so much for one of the best evenings ever," I say, breaking our embrace. "Drive safe."

"You too, Charlie."

Arriving at home, I can't get this stupid grin off my face. I already started to fall in love with him over the phone, but actually seeing him confirmed that feeling and now it feels deeper. Why didn't he kiss me, though? The moment was perfect. Maybe I should have initiated it? No, I don't think so, he doesn't come across unsure whatsoever, if anything, he looks as if he likes to call the shots. Not that he was pushy or anything, it's something about his mannerism that gives me the impression. Who knows, I could be wrong. Jumping into the shower, I let the hot water run down my body, closing my eyes, lost in him. Something about the way he held my hand makes me long for more. Images of his eyes fixated on me run through my mind, and I find myself running my hand over my breasts, wishing it were his. Traveling further down, I stop between my legs, massaging my already overly sensitive clit. I've been throbbing since the moment we locked eyes, and to be honest, a kiss would have just made it worse. With my head back, my fingers move faster, and I find myself close to orgasm. Suddenly, my phone ringing rips me out of my trance, and I turn off the shower, grab my towel, and wrap it around me. Rushing out, I reach it just in time, and I'm happy I didn't' miss the call. It's Xander.

Charlie: Hey!

Xander: Hi, Charlie. Just made it back to the hotel. Are you busy?

Charlie: Not at all.

Xander: This may sound crazy, but I missed you the second you drove away.

Hearing him say he misses me gives me a feeling I can't even begin to explain. His words make up for the aching buildup I feel in my groin, and the longer we talk, the more it fades, until it completely disappears.

Xander

Sitting in my hotel, my thoughts drift to Charlie and our date. So that was it, that was her. Wow, I can't believe it. She is even more stunning in person than on her pictures. Looking down at my hand, the pad of my thumb brushes the tips of my fingers, remembering exactly how her skin felt. I can still smell her scent, so sweet and innocent, just like her eyes. Even though her eyes are beautiful and stunning, they aren't her best feature. To me, it's her soul, it's so pure and clean, but I can feel a sort of pain buried deep down inside. I did notice about four or five scars on her right arm, and as curious as I was, I decided not to investigate. She will tell me when the time is right.

Getting up, I walk to the large window in my room and stare outside. Do I really want to pull her into this lifestyle? Wouldn't I be destroying that purity and innocence that fascinates me? I knew she was sweet, I picked up on that early on, but after meeting her, I'm not so sure I can go through with making her my sub. Xander, Xander, Xander, what in the hell have you started? You know you can't let up on her... actually, you know you won't.

Sitting on the sofa, I lean back and close my eyes. I already know that I can't just be friends with her. How did this even start? Oh yeah, with a message, a simple welcome message on my part after accepting her friend request. Un-fucking-believable. Each time we talk or chat, it just confirms how enamored I am with her and that it feels as if we are meant to be.

Opening my eyes, I feel torn. There is no way this woman is made for a Dom/sub relationship. I doubt she would let me take the lead, and there is no way she would obey any of my rules. Well, maybe if we both created them? Nope, I don't think so. Can I picture myself going vanilla? After all of these years?

Chapter 10

Charlie

"So, Charlie, how was your date?" Brynn asks while dunking her tortilla chip in way too much salsa.

"How did you know?" I ask, as the waiter refills my water. "Thank you."

"I may have let something slip," Leah confesses, biting her lip.

"Why am I not on the same page?" Rachel asks. "Charlie had a date?"

"Oh, god!" I say, leaning back against the leather padding of the booth.

"Yeah, she did, but she wants to keep his identity hush-hush for some reason," Leah teases. "The guy must be married or something."

"He's not," I reply with a bit of an attitude. "I'm not keeping it a secret. I just don't want you stalking him."

"Well, Leah," Brynn starts. "You have to admit; you are the first to send a friend request to someone we haven't even been out on a date with."

"True," Leah sighs. "I just want to make sure they are good guys. You know I'm like your guys' second mother."

With that statement, she gets an eye-roll from all of us in unison.

"Alright, alright. I'll back off a bit. Charlie, I swear I won't send him a friend request. I won't message him either. I swear to god, even if I don't believe in one."

"You don't have to. You're already friends with him anyway," I say, and her eyes widen. "It's X."

"X?" Brynn comments. "What kind of name is that?"

"Oh my god. No way!" Leah says with her mouth wide open. "The Author X?"

"Yep," I say, and then the waiter comes back to the table, setting our food in front of us.

"You sneaky bitch," Leah laughs. "I was wondering why you were suddenly showing up at his takeovers, acting like you are the best of friends."

"Sneaky bitch, huh?" I say.

"I'm just joking. You know I love you. Wow, I'm a little speechless but happy at the same time, he's such a great guy Charlie," Leah smiles. "I promise you I won't butt in or anything."

"Ok, someone better start from the beginning. X, takeover, what the hell are we talking about?" Rachel asks, clueless.

After filling her in on what takeovers are, she immediately asks what groups she should join. She's actually kind of upset that we've been holding out on her. She's an avid reader, and after finding out she can possibly connect with authors, she's over the moon.

"When are you seeing him again?" Brynn asks.

"Well, he lives in Ocean City. Not exactly close," I sigh.

"Wait!" Rachel interrupts. "Remember we wanted to take a weekend trip there months ago? Let's do it."

"I'm sure Charlie wants all of us to tag along on her date," Brynn says, rolling her eyes.

"Yeah, please don't," I reply.

"Of course not. Since we're there, it will make it easy to set something up with him."

"You're right," I say. "Kind of perfect."

"Let's go with next weekend," Leah suggests, and we all agree.

Next Friday is the last day of school before summer so I won't have to worry about preparing things for class. I am so excited to possibly see him again. Let's hope he doesn't already have plans. When I get home that night, I message Xander to see if he has time to talk. What a stupid question, he asked me to call him when I got back anyway. So, before he can reply, I hit the call button.

Xander: Hey, gorgeous. How was dinner?

Charlie: It was really nice. Hey, I have a question.

Xander: Shoot.

Charlie: What are you doing next weekend?

Xander: I was invited to an event on Saturday. Why?

Charlie: Damn.

Xander: Why? What's up?

Charlie: Well, my friends and I were planning a trip to Ocean City next weekend, and I was hoping you, and I could meet up and maybe go to dinner.

Xander: Yes! Let's do that. I've been dying to see you again.

Charlie: But I thought you had plans?

Xander: Well, I just got an offer I can't refuse. Consider them canceled.

Of course, this next week goes by so slow. The building anticipation of seeing Xander is slowly killing me. My poor students feel the same way, different reasons, of course. Three more days until summer vacation, and they are having a hard time sitting still in their seats. Since they are so hardworking and completed all of their tasks ahead of schedule for most of the year, I was able to get approval for a field trip to the aquarium tomorrow. Since Brynn works there, she was able to get everyone a deep discount on the tickets, and the chaperones get to go in free. As I sit in class while the children are drawing, my mind drifts to the upcoming weekend. Some of the thoughts are definitely less than appropriate for the setting I am in right now.

"Miss Harris! My pencil isn't working," Bella sulks, and I get up to walk toward her desk, thankful for the distraction.

Xander

I'm already looking forward to next weekend. Sure, I did have plans, a BDSM Event in Philadelphia, but I wouldn't miss the chance to spend time with Charlie. I feel as if we've grown even closer, and I know at one point I will have to confess who I am, though I'm not sure it will happen at our next meeting. I will have to feel things out. The last thing I want is for her to think I'm disturbed and run for the hills. This feeling of uncertainty is very new to me, though I know one thing, I don't want to let her slip through my fingers. I will just have to wait for the right time. Patience is one of my strong attributes.

Sitting at my desk, I check the time in the bottom right-hand corner of the screen, and thankfully, my workday is done, well partially. Now it's time to write the next chapter of my current work in progress, which still remains without a title. Another new thing for me, I usually have the title figured out before finishing Chapter One. To be quite honest, this whole entire book has proven to be a challenge. Maybe it's because it's a sequel, maybe it's just the constant writer's block, or maybe it's because my mind is somewhere else, actually, with someone else.

After about forty minutes of staring at the blinking cursor, I decide to call it a day, no use in forcing something that just isn't there. In my experience, I end up deleting most of those portions anyway, so it really is just a waste of time. Sure, I'm on a deadline with my publisher, but thankfully, they cut me a little slack from time to time.

A few minutes later, I receive a message from my friend Shawn, asking if I'm up to visiting Apex tonight and I figure why not, it's not like I'm going to write anyway. A change of scenery may get the wheels turning. Apex is a BDSM club not too far from where I live. It's not very large, but we always have a good time there.

After arriving at the club, Shawn and I are joined by two of our other friends, Max, and Nathan, along with their subs Roxanne and Samantha, and we take a seat on the plush sofas in the lounge after grabbing some drinks. My eyes peer toward the bar, and I notice a woman that has been looking in my direction since we arrived. I've seen her a few times in the past, never in the company of a Dom. Her lack of a collar is another indicator that she is available. Right as I am in the middle of a conversation with Max, I glance to my right and take notice that the woman from the bar is standing there, patiently waiting for me to acknowledge her.

"Yes," I say.

"Hello, my name is Luisa. May I ask yours?"

"You may. My name is Xander."

"Xander, it's a pleasure to meet you," Luisa replies smiling, her fingers playing with the lacy part of her corset right below her bulging breasts.

"Luisa, why don't you take a seat here between us," Shawn says patting the cushion of the sofa and within a second, she is wedged between us, one leg crossed over the other.

This is typical Shawn. He has been on the hunt for a sub for quite some time now. Shawn is a great guy, really nice guy, to be exact. It's just what he's into that isn't everybody's thing. Right as our group is in the middle of a discussion involving caning, I give my two cents, and an excited Luisa's hand rests on my thigh, unwelcomed.

"I love caning," she starts. "Xander, how about you and I sneak off and play?"

"I'm not here to play tonight," I respond, and she gives me a frown.

"Oh, come on. I'll make it worth your while," she smiles, and I politely decline again. If she asks again, I won't be so nice.

"I'd love to play with you, Luisa," Shawn offers, and Luisa gives me one more look that I just end up ignoring.

"All right, let's go," she says, and both get up to walk away.

"Looks like she wasn't going to let up," Nathan laughs, and I roll my eyes.

Don't get me wrong, normally I would love to use that cane and have some fun, but I'm just not in the mood tonight. Besides, Luisa didn't seem like the type that just wanted to play, she's definitely on the hunt for a Dom, and there is no way in hell I would consider, even if I hadn't met Charlie. About fifteen minutes later, Shawn returns with a drink in hand, sitting back down next to me.

"Wow, that was fast," Max comments as Shawn sits down.

"Waste of time. Right as I was about to tie her to the table, she came up with so many ridiculous excuses as to why she couldn't go through with it. I don't even think she is in the lifestyle."

"Damn, so she didn't get to experience any of your degrading?" I ask, knowing it's his thing.

"Oh, not to worry, I made sure she had a memorable departure."

"What did you say?" I ask, thinking he probably scarred the poor girl for life.

"Oh, nothing too bad, I just called her a cheap dirty little fuckwhore, and said she better run home before I bring her to her knees and face-fuck that filthy mouth of hers."

"Well, if you said it any different, it wouldn't be you," Nathan's sub, Samantha, chimes in and we all start to laugh.

Chapter 11

Charlie

It's 10 pm, and we finally arrived in Ocean City. Since we are splitting the cost between the four of us, we opted for an upscale hotel directly on the beach. After checking in, we walk toward the elevator, which takes us to the fourth floor. Walking down the long hall with our bags in tow, we finally reach our room and I throw myself on the bed. Since we all wanted to be in the same room, it means we will be sharing the two beds between the four of us but that's ok, we've done it before. Getting up from the bed, I pick up my purse from the floor to get my phone.

Xander,

We've arrived! Better late than never! I can't wait to see you tomorrow!

Charlie

Part of me wishes I could see him tonight, but it's already late, and I look like hell.

Charlie,

Glad you made it. Found the perfect place for lunch, you'll love it. I'll pick you up at noon. What's your room number?

Xander

The perfect place? I'm curious where he will be taking me. I'm sure it will be amazing.

Xander,

Room 404. Ready to meet the gang? lol

Charlie

I already told the girls they better be on their best behavior, especially Leah.

Charlie,

Anything for you gorgeous. Now get some rest! Maybe we will meet in our dreams.

Xander

The last message put a smile on my face that I know I will feel until the next day. After brushing my teeth, I get into bed, which by the way, I end up sharing with cover hog Rachel and drift off.

The four of us wake up early, go downstairs to grab some breakfast and take it back to the room to enjoy it on our private balcony.

"This is the life," Brynn says, enjoying the early rays of sunshine hitting her face.

"I agree," Leah replies, taking a bite of her watermelon. "I've always wanted to live at the beach."

"Hey Charlie, does X have a house on the beach?" Rachel asks curiously. Yes, I still haven't revealed his name to them, even though they've been poking and prodding.

"He does!" I reply. "Beautiful view. "Once in a while, he will send me pictures of the sunset."

"Romantic guy, huh?" Brynn comments, wiggling her eyebrows.

"He's very sweet," I say, taking a sip of my coffee.

Since we have plenty of time to spare, we take a walk on the beach, which turns into snapping about a million pictures of each other. We stop and sit on the sand, taking in the breeze on this otherwise hot day. Looking out into the distance, I let my mind go blank and just enjoy the sound of the seagulls and waves hitting the shore.

"Charlie, it's 11 am, we better get back," Leah screeches.

"Crap, I still have to shower," I say, getting up and brushing the sand off my legs.

Rushing back to the hotel, which takes us about fifteen minutes, I hurry into the shower, washing the rest of the sand off me. Getting out, I wrap the towel around me and quickly dry my hair. As I put on my make-up, I hear a loud knock at the door and freeze. Fuck, he's already here, and I'm not even dressed. Even worse? My clothes are on my bed. Standing in the bathroom, wrapped in only my towel, I grab my phone and message Leah, asking her to bring my clothes to me. Hearing my friends converse with him almost makes me lose hope that Leah will even see my text, especially since she is a big fan of his. Well, I have two options: one, text one of the others. Two, woman up and just walk out and get my clothes. I'm sure he's seen a woman in a towel before. What am I saying? Of course, he has. Option two it is. Opening the door, I step out and make sure to hold the part of the towel that is tucked in over my chest. The last thing I need is to stumble over something and the towel to hit the floor. It takes about five seconds before all eyes are on me.

"Hey guys," I say, feeling my cheeks burn at the sight of Xander standing there.

"Oh shit, your clothes," Leah comments. "Why didn't you call me to bring them to you."

"I texted you," I reply. "Sorry Xander, I'll be ready in just a second."

"Take your time Charlie," he smiles, never removing his eyes from me.

Rushing back into the bathroom, I try to hurry, but the more I rush, the longer it takes. Why is it taking me four tries to hook my damn bra? Deep breath Charlie...got it, finally. Once I'm dressed, a quick spritz of perfume, and I'm done. Stepping back out of the bathroom, I am again met with that devilish smile, and I walk up to give him a hug.

"So, I assume you've met everyone," I say, not wanting to let him go.

"I have," he replies. "The stories they've told me."

"Stories? Are you serious?" I say, my glance directed at Leah.

"I'm just kidding. You were gone for less than five minutes. They couldn't do too much damage."

"Lucky me," I sigh. "Are you ready?"

"I am," he replies, grabbing my hand. "It was great to meet you guys."

Walking out of the hotel, Xander informs me that the restaurant isn't very far from here, so we decide to walk. He wasn't joking. It's less than half a mile down the road. It looks to be a seafood place, which has me super excited because I love seafood. Once the hostess shows us to our table, Xander pulls out my chair before walking around to the other side to take his seat. Making our selections, the waiter takes our orders and disappears into the kitchen. The restaurant is very small, almost like one of those hole in the wall places. In my experience, those are some of the best.

"I'm so happy you're here Charlie," Xander says, grabbing my hand across the table.

"Me too, I'm sorry that it happened to be the weekend you originally had something planned. What kind of event was it?"

"Umm...nothing important. Just this annual thing where I meet up with some friends. But really, don't worry about it, I wasn't really feeling it anyway," he says, and I can't shake the feeling as if he is keeping something from me.

"So, do you live close to here?" I ask, and he nods.

"Yes, about five minutes south of here. "I'm sure you're happy to have a break from work."

"Oh god, yes, I am," I reply. "Though I will say I really enjoyed my time with these students, and I think I will miss them."

"You like kids then?" he asks.

"I do, how about you?" I counter.

"I do, I think," he chuckles. "To be honest, I've never really wasted much of a thought on actually having one, but with the right woman, maybe two."

"Same here, though when I was younger, I thought I always wanted four," I smile.

"The more, the merrier," he jokes, taking a drink of his water.

"You don't drink, do you?" I ask, and he swallows.

"Not really, maybe three times a year or for special occasions. Not really for me, I don't like to lose control," he explains.

"Makes sense, some of the things people do when drunk are definitely questionable," I smile.

"I think we are back to playing the question game," he points out, and I grin because we always seem to be playing this game.

"Speaking of the question game, have you seriously never been in love?" I ask, curiously.

"I have not," he replies.

"But you've had relationships."

"I have, very good ones too," he adds.

"But you've never loved them? That blows my mind; how does that happen?"

"I loved them in a different way. I have yet to meet the person that gives me the feeling of home. My Ex...girlfriends were wonderful for the most part, but it just wasn't real love. If it were, I wouldn't be single right now."

"Well, I guess you're right about that," I say, thinking about what he said.

"To be honest, I believe a great love comes once in a lifetime. You may feel as if you've been in love, and maybe you have, but it takes a special person to really claim your heart. Sure, we are compatible with many different people, and more than likely, many of those relationships would work, but I'm searching for more."

"Interesting," I say, letting it all sink it.

"Think about it. You've had boyfriends before, right?"

"Of course," I reply.

"Let's talk about your last boyfriend. What made you guys split up?"

"Nothing specific. We moved to Baltimore, and the first three months were great since it was just the two of us. He was very involved with his job, and after some time, we drifted apart," I admit.

"You drifted apart. The communication was gone."

"Yes, we definitely stopped talking," I say, recalling that time, remembering feeling as if I lived with a stranger.

"I believe when you meet the one, you're destined to be with, that does not happen. The love you share trumps everything, and you fight to keep it alive, always. You never stop communicating. It's so important," he says. "Once you stop communicating, the walls begin to crack. If you're not careful, the walls will continue to crack until they collapse."

"Wow, I never thought of it that way," I say.

"Most couples love repairing with band-aids, hoping that things will fix themselves. The problems never fix themselves, and after a while, things fall apart, and people become bitter. I don't fix things with band-aids. I search for the root of the problem, mending it before it even has a chance to start cracking. Though, in order for this to happen, you have to find your match."

"Well, in a perfect world," I reply.

"In my world," he counters, looking directly at me.

At that moment, our food arrives, and the conversation changes course to something less profound. Maybe it's the writer in him; it sounded so poetic. He's right, though; communication is the key. I think that's why I find myself falling in love with Xander. We talk about everything, and I can tell he truly cares. After lunch, we take a stroll on the beach, walking for hours, talking. Once we make it back to the hotel, we stop in the lobby, and I ask if he would like to come upstairs.

"I'd love to," he replies, squeezing my hand tighter.

"Phew, I'm glad my friends didn't scare you off," I joke.

"It takes much more than that," he replies, smirking, and suddenly, I don't have a response, except for a coy smile.

Walking down the hall, we reach the room, and I stick the keycard into the slot, but I just get a red flashing light. I try again, getting a little frazzled with each attempt before I feel Xander's hand on mine.

"Wrong side," he comments and turns the card around, sticking it in the slot, and what do you know, green light.

"Wow, I feel like an idiot," I say under my breath.

"You're just nervous, I can tell. Though I'm not sure why. I noticed it as soon as we got into the elevator."

Damn, I thought I was doing good disguising myself, well then again, sticking the keycard in frantically without checking the directing pretty much gives it all away. Let's hope the girls don't reveal all of my embarrassing stories.

Xander

As we step into the room, Charlie announces our arrival, but we are met with silence. Walking further in, she sets her purse on a desk and scans the room.

"I guess they're not here," she replies and opens the blinds to the balcony. "Do you want to sit outside?"

"Sure," I say as she opens the sliding glass door, following her outside.

Charlie walks to the railing and looks out to the ocean, a smile on her face. The rays of the evening sun make her blue eyes seem even brighter.

"You know what's funny?" Charlie asks, looking at me.

"What?"

"I have never met anyone from the internet in person before," she replies, and I smile. "I never had the desire to."

"What was the turning point?" I ask, and she raises an eyebrow. "What made you want to meet me?"

"I've never felt this connected to a person before. I feel like I can tell you everything, and you won't judge me. You definitely know more about me than most people."

"I will never judge you," I reply, and she grabs my hand and holds it.

"I think you taking control and telling me that you were going to be in Baltimore and wanted us to meet, took a little pressure off me. I knew I wanted to meet you but didn't know how to go for it," she admits, and I feel my heart beat faster.

"You don't like to be in control?" I ask, and she thinks for a moment.

"It depends, I'm in control when I teach, and I enjoy it, but sometimes I just don't want to think or make decisions. I can be unsure of things and question them to no end as well."

"Is that something you want to work on?" I ask, stroking her hand with my thumb.

"Yes, and no," she replies. "Yes, because I need to be more decisive and no because that's my personality."

"Indecisiveness at its finest right there," I chuckle. "The key is not to lose who you are, just tweak things little by little. Best advice I can give you when it comes to making decisions is to go with your gut."

"You're right. So instead of wondering for three minutes if I want mustard or ketchup on my hot dog, I should just go with the first thing that pops in my mind," she smiles, and I give myself a faceplant.

"Ketchup or mustard? Really? I thought they were difficult decisions," I joke, and she starts to laugh.

"Well, depending on my mood, it can make or break the flavor of the hot dog," she teases, and I shake my head.

"Just eliminate the hot dog," I reply.

"That may be a good idea."

For a moment, there is a silence between us, only our eyes communicating. She looks vulnerable yet wanting. She likes the feeling of someone taking control? That's what I will do. Placing my hand on the back of her neck, I pull her lips close to mine and kiss her softly. Her hand touches my cheek, and she returns the kiss. Her lips are soft, and she tastes of everything I crave. My grip becomes a bit harder, and my kiss more demanding, my tongue invading her mouth to dance with hers. She responds with the same urgency, and second later, we are lost in each other. My hand moves up to her hair, and it takes everything in me not to grab a fistful, moving her head to the side to expose her neck to leave a trail of bites. Slowing down, I eventually break the kiss and hold her in my arms: discipline, Xander, discipline.

Chapter 12

Charlie

It's been two weeks since Ocean City, but I still find myself daydreaming about that kiss we shared. When I close my eyes, I relive that moment, his hand on the back of my neck, his scent, everything about him. Xander and I still talk every single day, multiple times, actually. His workload has been a bit demanding over the last week, so our conversations had to be cut short a few times. As I stand in line at the grocery store, my phone chimes, and I smile when I see his name.

Charlie,

Hey! Finally finished working for the day and I'm beat. Wanted to see if you had any plans this weekend?

Xander

This weekend? Is he going to be in town?

Xander

I'm free this weekend. Why? Do you want to come see me?

Charlie

Fingers crossed; I miss him.

Charlie,

Yes!! So, here's the plan. I was thinking of leaving Ocean City on Saturday morning, and we could meet for lunch and maybe walk around the city for a bit.
Unfortunately, I have to leave that night because I've

already promised to help a friend of mine move some things on Sunday morning. I've missed you and really want to see you.

Xander

I re-read that message at least a dozen times, my smile growing bigger and bigger.

Xander,

I've missed you too. I would love that. Would it be easier if I just come there? I'd hate for you to do all that driving.

Charlie

Hanging out at the beach sounds like a great idea to me.

Charlie,

You are the sweetest. Nope, I'm coming there. If you'll have me.

Xander

If I'll have him? Is he serious? If I could, I'd never let him go again. I swear, I found my perfect match. Sure, I may be premature in my assumption since we've only met twice, but all those hours on the phone, all the messages. I feel like we know everything there is to know about one another. Two more days! I can't wait.

I spend Friday night at a local bar with the girls, catching up. Since Brynn and Ryan have started dating, we've seen less of her, which is totally understandable.

"Yeah, so we've been talking about moving in together," Brynn starts. "I know we haven't known each other that long but we click."

"How do you and his daughter get along?" Rachel asks.

"Really good actually, which surprises me since I'm not really into kids, but his little girl is a sweetheart. So, Charlie, how are things with Xander?"

"Great!" I begin. "I get to see him tomorrow, actually. He's driving here to visit."

"Oh, that's great!" Leah smiles. "Do you think you can get him to sign my book for me? I meant to bring it to Ocean City but forgot."

"Are you serious?" I say, looking at her like she's lost her mind, but her hopeful eyes reveal she is not joking. "All right, bring it by in the morning."

About three hours and quite a few drinks later, we call it a night and I wait for my cab. On the ride home, I send Xander a text, telling him I can't wait to see him and that I am super excited. Immediately, he replies, sending me a smiley face.

The next day, I'm awoken by a cheery Leah standing in front of my door, handing over the book she wants Xander to sign. I honestly didn't think she would make it, especially with the amount of alcohol she consumed the night before. Standing in my bathroom, I turn on the shower, and as I wait for the water to heat, I brush my teeth. While washing my hair, I make a mental note on what I have in my closet, and since the weather has been very nice, I opt for a dress today. Nothing too fancy, it's just lunch anyway.

As I get out of the shower, my phone chimes, and I notice it's a message from Xander saying he will be here in about twenty minutes. We were going to meet at the restaurant, but since it's really close to my apartment, I told him to just meet me here. It's literally five minutes away, so it would be silly to use cars.

Taking one last look into the mirror in my bathroom, I retouch my mascara when I hear the doorbell ring. Damn, he's early! Rushing to the front door, I open it, melting immediately. His smile, his eyes...everything. He steps towards me and, without words, places the palm of his hand on my cheek, kissing me, and once again, I'm lost in him. As we break the kiss, all we can do is smile at each other, and then I realize he's still standing in the doorway, so I ask him to come inside.

"You look beautiful," Xander says, grabbing my hand and squeezing it once more before releasing it again.

"Thank you so much," I reply. "You look handsome as ever and smell amazing."

"New cologne," he says, winking at me before looking around the living room. "I like your place, very nice."

"Thank you. It's a little small, but it's home," I reply, grabbing my shoes from the coat closet. "So, traffic must have been alright on the way here?"

"It was, surprisingly. I figured with it being Saturday, it could be a little dicey, but it looks as though everyone was heading in the other direction."

After I grab my purse, we head out and make our way down the stairs. Once at the bottom, Xander grabs my hand, and we walk in the direction of the restaurant. Like I said, it's very close and we make it there in no time. As the hostess asks if we would like to be seated inside or outside, we opt for outdoors since the weather couldn't be any better. After ordering our meals, Xander and I are lost in conversation, ranging from the current book he is writing to some of the most embarrassing moments we've ever had. I love how affectionate he is, holding my hand any chance he gets, even from across the table. After we finish eating, the waiter brings the bill, and Xander snatches it up in a snap.

"Not fair," I say. "I thought we agreed I'm paying this time?"

"There was no agreement," he smiles, placing his credit card into the holder, and I playfully pout.

"Sassy, huh?" he comments.

"Well, Xander, by the smile on your face, it seems to me that you enjoy sassiness," I reply, and he bites his lip as if he's holding back a comment.

"You have no idea, Charlie," he then replies. "You have no idea."

Leaving the restaurant, we take a walk around downtown, immersed in conversation, and taking the occasional selfie together. I can't believe how fast time flies when you don't want it to. Since Xander has to drive back to Ocean City today, we make our way back to my apartment, and I ask if he'd like to come back upstairs before leaving.

Once inside, I take off my shoes, and Xander does the same, taking a seat on the couch. Going into the kitchen, I return with two glasses of water, setting them on the coffee table. Xander reaches for my hand, pulling me toward him on the couch.

"Hours seem like seconds when I spend them with you," he comments, kissing my forehead.

"I agree," I sigh. "I really wish you could stay."

"Charlie?"

"Yes?" I reply, looking at him.

"I really like you," he pauses. "A lot!"

"I really like you too," I smile, and he looks as if he's thinking about something.

"I need to be honest with you. Even though we live a few hours apart, I really would love to take this to the next level," he explains, and I am screaming for joy inside.

"I feel the same way," I respond, and he squeezes my hand and kisses my lips before pulling away, looking as if he has something to say.

"I have a confession to make," he pauses for a few seconds. "Charlie, I love in a different way."

"Okay? What do you mean?" I ask.

"What I mean is I'm not your typical guy when it comes to intimacy," he replies, and I wonder what he could be talking about. "What I do isn't considered the norm for most people."

"Don't tell me you're into whips and chains," I chuckle, and he smiles.

"Well, there's way more to it," he says, looking directly into my eyes.

"You're messing with me, aren't you?" I ask, and his silence gives the answer. What the fuck? "So, you're into kinky things?"

"Well," he begins. "I mean sure, there's kink involved but it's more than that."

"Like handcuffs?" I ask.

"Of course, but I prefer rope," he chuckles. "More options."

"More options?"

"Yes. Not so easy to tie your elbows or legs with handcuffs," he counters, and I'm speechless for a moment.

"You said there's way more to it. What exactly is *IT* if I may ask?"

"I practice BDSM," he replies. "I'm a Dominant."

"BDSM? As in you like to hurt people?"

"No! Not at all," he corrects me. "It's all about trust and communication."

"Trust that you aren't going to kill me?" I say, feeling myself fall apart a little inside, knowing that he and I aren't compatible.

"Trust that I know how far to push you, what your boundaries are," he says. "I would never hurt you."

"Wow," I say, being at a loss for words. After my initial shock, I manage to ask a few questions. "I don't really know anything about it except for what I saw in movies, can you tell me why you chose this lifestyle?"

"I was introduced to BDSM by a former girlfriend twelve years ago, and that's when I became intrigued. At that time, we only lived our fantasies in the bedroom. It wasn't until much later that I found out about all of the different lifestyles that exist within this community. After years and years of learning, I finally found my niche and became a lifestyle, Dom."

"What is a lifestyle, Dom?"

"I am a dominant man by nature, and I love living this dominant side twenty-four hours a day, seven days a week. No breaks," he replies.

"Can you give me an example?" I ask, curiosity driving me.

"An example?" he asks. "Um, alright. Let's say you and I are together, I will be giving you challenges, tasks, or asking for favors, and I will expect them to be done right on time. If you don't complete them, you would get punished."

"Did you have a bad childhood?" I ask, hoping I'm not crossing a line.

"No," he laughs. "I know it's the stereotype. I had a happy childhood and have a wonderful relationship with my mom. My dad died a few years ago like I told you, but we were close as well."

"Does she know what you do?"

"Oh, no," he replies. "I don't go around announcing this to everyone. Most people won't react positively, so I pick and choose who I tell."

"And you chose to tell me," I say, looking at my hands.

"Yes, because I see a future with you. I want a future with you," he begins. "Listen, I know it's a lot to take in, and I don't expect you to jump at me and say you're ok with everything. If you decide to open yourself up to this lifestyle, to learn, to explore, you'll come to find out it's a very slow process. Don't feel as if you're rushed into anything."

"Xander," I begin.

"Charlie?"

"Can I ask you something else?"

"Of course," he replies, his eyes studying me.

"So, you aren't interested in a girlfriend. You're just looking for women to dominate?"

"No!" he says quickly. "You would be my partner. As my partner, you will also be my submissive."

"Submissive?"

"Yes," he replies.

"You want me to submit to everything you tell me to do? What if it's something I'm uncomfortable with?"

"Like I said, it's a very slow process that starts with vetting time. It's where we really get to know one another inside and out, likes, dislikes, soft limits, hard limits."

"How many submissive's have you had?"

"I've had three," he replies, and I, for some reason, figured it would be a higher number.

"Do they all start out like me? Totally clueless?"

"Not at all. I usually meet potential subs through friends or at a dungeon. All three have already been in the lifestyle. The way you and I came to be is completely new to me."

"What is a dungeon?" I ask, a little afraid.

"A dungeon?" he smiles. "It's what we call a **BDSM** club."

"Xander, can I be honest?"

"Yes. Always!"

"I don't think that is the kind of relationship I am looking for. I can't imagine myself being ok with any of that stuff," I reply, and I can see his eyes reflect a hint of sadness.

"I understand you feeling that way, especially not knowing anything about it. It's a lot to take in, but all I ask is that you think about it and please ask me questions. Any fears or concerns you have; I will try to take away. Communication is the basis of this relationship. We have to be open with each other and honest at all times."

"You're right. This is a lot to take in," I say. "I think if you'd tell me you had a criminal record, I'd be less shocked."

"You're kidding me, right?"

"Yeah," I chuckle. "I'm just messing with you."

"There was a little laugh. I hope you will at least consider thinking about it?"

"Well," I take a deep breath. "All right. I will think about it. I can't make you any promises, though."

"I don't expect you to," he replies, squeezing my hand. "In the meantime, please, ask me anything you'd like to know. Knowing you, as soon as I leave, you will be researching on your laptop."

"Damn, how did you know?"

"A feeling I had," he smiles, and I roll my eyes. "I just want to make sure you have the right information, so please utilize me as your resource."

"Ok, I will," I smile, and he leans in, kissing my forehead.

Xander

Well, this wasn't the reaction I was hoping for. Disappointing, I must admit. I do understand her though, her mixed emotions and fears. It's not like she's choosing between chocolate and vanilla ice cream here. Did I not make it sound intriguing? Did I explain myself poorly?

Entering my house, I walk into the kitchen and throw my keys on the kitchen island. Well, that was the end of that. She will deny me and everything I was hoping for, everything I wanted to share with her. I can't be angry, though; this lifestyle isn't for everyone. It takes real dedication and will to endure the first steps into it. You can't fake it. It won't get you anywhere. I suppose I can only hope that she is willing to give this a try, it's out of my hands for now.

As I pour myself a glass of tea, I recall the moment Charlie brought up the part about hurting people. If she only knew. Why does everyone automatically steer directly to the pain of it? If people would just know that there is so much more to experience.

What am I supposed to do if she denies me? Walk away? Change my life? Hell, I don't know if I could just walk away.

Chapter 13

Charlie

Wow, that was a confession I wasn't expecting. I'm still not quite sure how I feel about it. My gut is telling me to cut ties here and forget about any kind of future with him. I would be insane for even considering this kind of relationship. My mind is intrigued, wondering what this part of his life is about. My heart? Well, my heart already belongs to him. I know we've only met a few times, but with all of the hours we've talked on chat and the phone, I know him too well to just walk away.

Grabbing my laptop, I begin my research. Clicking on the internet icon, I type **BDSM** into the search bar and hit enter. Well, I suppose I will start with the first link. After reading through the first few paragraphs, I notice a glossary of terms off to the side and click that link. Edging, Fisting, Knife Play, Master/Slave, Breath Play...the list goes on and on, and my eyes keep getting wider and wider. Next, I make a big mistake. I click on the video tab and watch a woman that is gagged and tied to a table getting hit with some sort of stick. Part of me wants to close the window, but I can't get myself to do it. Here is this woman, her ass shining red, makeup running down her face, muffled screams...how in the hell is she enjoying herself? I mean, sure I can see how the guy might be having fun in some sort of sick way, but there is no way she is getting any kind of pleasure out of this. After spending about thirty more minutes on a few different sites, I shut the laptop and sit back in the chair. How can someone like Xander be into this? He had to have been joking. Is he really a sadist? Well, actually, this would be a great question to ask him. Apparently, there are different types of Doms, and they aren't all into the same things. I think Xander is right, and I need to utilize him as a resource instead of assuming what I am reading is correct. Suddenly, my phone chimes, and I already know who it is.

Charlie,

Just wanted to let you know that I made it back. Hope I didn't scare you away. I always want to be honest with you, and I hope you will do the same with me. Call tomorrow?

Xander

His message brings a smile to my face, like I said, he already has my heart. Now I just need to figure out if and how we will be compatible in this department.

Waking up the next morning, I feel well rested even though I tossed and turned most of the night. Part of me wishes I would have just called him last night, I have so many questions, but don't know where to start. I know he said he had to help a friend move today, so maybe I can catch him beforehand. Grabbing my phone off the nightstand, I send him a good morning message to see if he's awake. In an instant, I get a reply, and I chuckle to myself. Why am I not surprised? This man never sleeps. My phone chimes again and he's asking if he can call me and I can't wait to talk to him. As my phone rings, complete horror hits me. He pressed video chat. Well, he's seen me with goop all over my face, bedhead won't be such a big deal, I guess.

Xander: Good morning, beautiful!

Charlie: Umm...I wasn't expecting a video call. You need to warn me before.

Xander: Why?

Charlie: Look at me!

Xander: I am, and I love what I see.

Charlie: Well, thank you. You look like you've been up for hours.

Xander: Yep, I have been. Just finished my run and I have about two hours before I have to meet my friend.

Charlie: Busy day then?

Xander: Oh yeah, definitely. So, let me guess. You did some research on the internet.

Charlie: Oh yeah.

Xander: Uh oh, and now you're terrified.

Charlie: Well, shocked, confused... maybe a little intrigued.

Xander: Well, I can work with that. At least you didn't say absolutely not.

Charlie: I just have some questions.

Xander: I would have been surprised if you didn't. I'm ready, shoot!

Charlie: Well, online I read something that there are different types of Doms. Which one are you?

Xander: Daddy Dom.

Charlie: What?

Xander: I'm just fucking with you. No, I'm a lifestyler.

Charlie: Oh, thank god. I could never picture myself calling you daddy. That's right, and you did mention that yesterday, I guess I forgot.

Xander: No worries, I hit you with quite the bomb yesterday.

Charlie: What exactly does lifestyler mean again?

Xander: It means I live my dominant nature 24 hours a day, every day.

Charlie: Oh, that's right; it's slowly coming back. You said something about challenges. Can you give me another example?

Xander: Alright. If you are my sub, I will check on you many times throughout the day.

Charlie: Check on me? Like, ask how my day is?

Xander: That too, but that's when I will give you tasks.

Charlie: Are tasks the same as challenges?

Xander: Not exactly.

Charlie: Can you give me an example of a task?

Xander: Of course. I may ask you to take a sexy picture of yourself and send it to me.

Charlie: What if I'm at work?

Xander: Doesn't matter.

Charlie: Doesn't matter? How the hell am I supposed to do that?

Xander: It's up to you to figure that out. Just know, I will never ask anything that is impossible.

Charlie: Well, what if I don't do it?

Xander: Then you'll get punished.

Charlie: Wow!

Xander: Wow?

Charlie: That's not really fair.

Xander: Why isn't it fair?

Charlie: I mean, if I am sitting here with a bunch of second graders, how am I supposed to complete a task?

Xander: I will know your schedule. Like I said. I won't ask anything that is impossible, and besides, we will have agreed to this beforehand.

Charlie: How can you punish me if you're so far away?

Xander: Believe me, I have my ways.

Charlie: Alright, what exactly do I get out of this?

Xander: You will discover a lot about yourself, learn your boundaries, your desires, your fears. I will be there with you every step of the way.

Charlie: You mentioned that this is a long process, and you said something about vetting time?

Xander: Yes, vetting time. I know we've already gotten to know a lot about each other, but during vetting time we will basically learn everything there is to know about one another, almost like stripping down to nothing. The most important thing is that we have to be honest with each other, no matter how uncomfortable it gets. It's the only way this works. I won't judge you; you can tell me anything and it stays with me.

Charlie: How will this work when we are so far apart?

Xander: Well, yeah, distance is an issue, more for the future though, but nothing is impossible.

Charlie: Alright.

Xander: So, does that mean you are interested in learning?

Charlie: One more thing.

Xander: Yes?

Charlie: I can quit whenever I want to?

Xander: Quit? Sometimes we have to start to get somewhere, right?

Charlie: True.

Xander: If you are uncomfortable, yes, definitely let me know. I won't force you to do anything you don't agree to. As a sub, you actually hold the reigns as well, when you say no, it's no, no matter how much I would want it. Honestly, I don't think you will quit.

Charlie: That's quite confident. What makes you say that?

Xander: I know you.

Charlie: All right. I will give it a shot.

Xander

Wow, she is going to be a project. She already asked if she could just quit at any time. She hasn't even started yet. Fuck my life! Well, at least she wasn't opposed to it, that's a good sign, right? I understand her concerns, she's new to this lifestyle, and I remember having doubts myself when I first joined.

My challenge will be giving her structure. She seems to doubt every single thing unless proven wrong. I walk into the kitchen to grab an apple and sit on the sofa, letting our conversation run through my head. I will stick to my plan. An educated sub would have been much easier, but I do like a challenge.

It's going to be a long journey with bumpy roads, but I'm determined to make her the best she can be and therefore, the best submissive I've ever had.

Chapter 14

Charlie

Today is the start of...well, I'm not exactly sure what to call it. My unconventional relationship with Xander? In any case, today is the start of something new, something that scares and excites me at the same time. I think it's the fear of the unknown that gets me. Putting all of my trust into someone else is very hard for me. I will give this my best shot, though. Xander called me after helping his friend move and laid out a few ground rules:

1) Honesty
2) Trust
3) Working together to create a strong bond

Sounds easy enough. I honestly thought the rules would be hard. Well, he did mention something about really disliking sassiness. That will be something I will struggle with. I can be a little sassy at times, and he's pointed it out several times. I really do believe that deep down, he enjoys it, though. Our phone conversation turned into another three hours session, where he explained exactly how we will get started. I must say I am actually looking forward to the tasks and challenges. He mentioned that some will be writing assignments, and I may wrangle with myself, but I'm up for it. I think it's best to have a positive outlook on this. Besides, I agreed to jump into it. During our conversation, Xander shared that he discovered early on that he had dominant tendencies and liked to call the shots. Learning the lifestyle took a lot of time, patience, and there were times he became frustrated, but quitting was never an option. To tell the truth, I wouldn't have expected anything less. He seems determined to succeed in anything he does.

After breakfast, I call my mom to see how things have been going there. As she talks about an upcoming church trip, I'm lost in thought. Wow, if my parents had any idea about the journey I am about to embark on, I'm sure they would dunk me in holy water and order some kind of an exorcism. I remember when they found out I had sex before marriage, what a lecture I got. It's like I burst all of their hopes and dreams. Luckily, they got over it, took about six months, and me accompanying them to every function they attended. I can see it now. *Hey mom and dad, meet my new boyfriend Xander, he's a Dom and likes to do things you wouldn't even imagine in your nightmares.* Well, I suppose I don't know what it is he actually likes to do, but I'm sure I will find out sooner than later.

Right in the middle of scrubbing my bathtub, I can hear my phone ring in the other room. Taking off my gloves, I run to answer it.

Charlie: Hey Xander, how are you?

Xander: Good. What are you doing?

Charlie: I was just cleaning my bathroom, nothing exciting.

Xander: Well, it has to be done. I have a question for you.

Charlie: All right, go ahead.

Xander: How often do you masturbate?

Charlie: What?

Xander: You heard me.

Charlie: Umm...that's very personal. I don't want to answer that.

Xander: Charlie...

Charlie: Yes?

Xander: What did we talk about?

Charlie: To be open and honest with each other.

Xander: How often?

Charlie: Oh my god, Xander, really?

Xander: Open and honest, Charlie. We are building trust, building a bond.

Charlie: It depends. Maybe three times a week?

Xander: Is that a question or a statement?

Charlie: Three times a week.

Xander: That's better. Do you use toys?

Charlie: Sometimes.

Xander: What do you have?

Charlie: Wow! Well, I have a wand and a dildo.

Xander: Good start.

Charlie: Can I ask you the same question?

Xander: Every day.

Charlie: Wow, you answered quickly.

Xander: I have nothing to hide. I want to share everything with you and want to learn all I can of you. Anyway, Charlie, from now on, you are not allowed to pleasure yourself unless you have my permission.

Charlie: Excuse me? So, I have to ask your permission?

Xander: Yes.

Charlie: Well, what if you're not available when I'm in the mood.

Xander: Then, you don't get to.

Charlie: You'll never know if I do.

Xander: First of all, that was sassy. I'll let that one slide for now, though. Second, I trust you, Charlie. I know you won't just disregard what I say.

Charlie: I'm sorry. I didn't mean to be sassy.

Xander: You are forgiven. I have to get back to work, but I have a task for you. I want you to write down your darkest fantasy and send it to me. You have until 8 pm tonight. Thank you.

Before I can say another word, he is gone. My darkest fantasy? Shouldn't be too hard. I go back to cleaning the bathroom, and as I scrub the toilet, my mind is blank. Do I have any dark fantasies? There has to be one floating around somewhere. I suppose I can make one up... no. I can't. Lying is not acceptable; I have to be honest. Next, my thoughts drift to our earlier conversation about masturbating. What does he get out of me, only touching myself when he says so? It's not like he's watching me or anything. Oh well, I better finish up my cleaning since I'm due to meet Leah for dinner in a few hours.

Walking into the little Mexican place on the corner, Leah gets up from the bench in the lobby and gives me a hug.

"Charlie!" she squeezes me tight. "Did you bring the book?"

"The book?" I ask, confused. "Oh my god, the book!"

"You didn't have him sign it?"

"Umm...crap, no, I forgot. Damn it. I'm so sorry, Leah," I apologize.

"The two of you must have been busy doing other things," she giggles before we walk up to the hostess to see about a table.

We are seated immediately, and a waiter sets a basket of chips and a bowl of queso on the table. How did I forget about the book? I'm such a terrible friend.

"So, did the two of you get it on?"

"No," I say, shaking my head. "Do you really think I give it up that easy?"

"Well, no, not normally, but Xander is not your normal kind of guy either," she swoons.

"You got that right," I smirk, and the waiter returns to take our order.

"Hey, Leah, what's your darkest fantasy?" I ask, thinking maybe she will give me a little inspiration.

"Being fucked by two guys at the same time," she replies, and my eyes widen. "I've thought about maybe three, but not sure if I can concentrate on sucking while I've got that going on."

"Are you completely serious?" I ask.

"Well, you said darkest fantasy, right? Yeah, that would be it. Will it ever happen? Probably not, but the thought definitely turns me on. What's yours?" she asks.

"I don't know. Definitely not that," I chuckle.

Once our food arrives, we dig in, and I can't get the image of Leah with three guys out of my head. Now I wish I hadn't asked in the first place. Who knows, maybe she would be better with someone like Xander, she's adventurous, way more than I am at least. I did read that multiple partners can play a role in this lifestyle. I suppose it depends on the Doms preference. This is definitely something I have to ask him. Even though I know I need to be open, I can't see myself sharing him with anyone. God, I hope he is more of the monogamous type. After paying for our dinner, I tell Leah I will make sure that I will get her book signed the next time I see Xander, and after giving me a hug, she walks toward her car. The restaurant isn't too far away from my place, so I opted to walk, spare the environment of unnecessary fumes.

When I get home, I look at the clock, and I have a little less than two hours before I have to complete my writing assignment. Xander has already messaged me several times today, a few times to see what I'm up to; other times, he sent me a funny meme or GIF. Every one of his messages sends a smile to my face, and if it were up to me, he could definitely continue. Sitting at my table, my phone in hand, I stare at the blank message screen in front of me. My darkest fantasy...I got it. I start typing away, and a few minutes later, I am confident that I did a good job, so I hit send. About two minutes later, my phone chimes, and Xander replied with one word - *cute.*

Great! What's that supposed to mean? As I try to type back a reply, my phone rings and speak of the devil, it's him.

Charlie: Cute?

Xander: Yes. That's what it was. I'm not sure if I should punish you for failing the task or give you this one for being honest and quite innocent.

Charlie: Hmm.

Xander: Being blindfolded is a start for sure; I wish you had taken it further.

Charlie: Further? How much further?

Xander: You want my version?

Charlie: Umm, do I? Will it be scary? I'm kidding, yes, I do.

Xander: I would have you blindfolded sitting in a chair. Wrists behind your back, tied to the back. Ankles restrained to the legs of the chair. Then you would hear me enter the room. I would stand directly in front of you, and you could hear the sound of my belt being removed. After snapping it once or twice, you would feel it around your neck... Charlie, are you still with me.

Charlie: Umm...yes.

Xander: Everything alright?

Charlie: Isn't that a little extreme?

Xander: Which part?

Charlie: Well, I don't like the idea of having my ankles tied up. Wrists are ok...I think. The belt around my neck? Hell no.

Xander: So, a no go?

Charlie: Oh, yes.

Xander: I can respect that. How do you feel about a collar?

Charlie: Like a dog collar?

Xander: No, not a dog collar, hold on. Let me send you a picture.

Charlie: Ok, I think I got it; let me check.

Xander: Sure.

Charlie: Well, even though it looks a little degrading, there is something beautiful about it.

Xander: It is beautiful.

Charlie: Why wear a collar? Is that the Pet Play I read about?

Xander: No, not at all. The collar in the picture I sent you is a training collar. The training collar is used as long as a sub is under consideration.

Charlie: Under consideration?

Xander: Yes. After the vetting comes consideration time. It's to see if the Dom and sub really fit together. The collar signifies that you are my sub if we happen to go out to a club. Obviously, it's used for play as well. I think you'd enjoy it.

Charlie: You think? Ok, so if you're not walking me around like a dog, what are you doing with it?

Xander: Many things. Here's an example. You're on your knees, and I want you to suck my cock. Instead of saying something, I will just pull the leash attached to the collar until your mouth is on it.

Charlie: Oh.

Xander: Another, if I'm fucking you from behind and I want you to move, by me pulling it, I set the pace. It's a lot of fun; I think you'd really enjoy it.

Charlie: Well, something to get used to, I guess.

Xander: Is that a yes on the collar?

Charlie: Maybe.

Xander: Great, maybe I can work with. By the way, no punishment. It's your fantasy. Though, I will still punish you for another matter.

Charlie: Another matter? What do you mean?

Xander: Let me refresh your memory. *Umm, do I? Will it be scary?*

Charlie: Sassy.

Xander: Yes.

Charlie: So, what is my punishment?

Xander: No social media for two days. Thank you.

Chapter 15

Charlie

I'm a month into this and so far, so good. The information he is giving me is plentiful, and I almost want to write everything down since I'm sure I will forget things here and there. Right now, I am working on another writing assignment. To be honest, I never imagined I would be doing so much writing. I suppose it's a great way to learn. Most of the assignments have been straightforward and easy, and I've passed every single one. This one I'm very confident about, he's asking me to write a **BDSM** scene by giving me three items, blindfold, crop and candles. My fingers are typing away. Thoughts entirely focused on how I will integrate these items and use them. About fifteen minutes later, I finish and send it to his email.

Having to make a quick trip to the post office, I figure now is as good as ever. While driving, my mom calls, and I click the green phone button on my steering wheel. Once she finds out I am driving, she raises her voice, and it blares over the speaker above me. For some reason, she thinks I can't understand her even though the thing is right above my head. I gave up telling her about it. I'm surprised to find out that they are planning on visiting me in two weeks, they have only been out here once, and Baltimore was definitely not their kind of city. I will admit, I do sometimes miss the sunshine in SoCal, laying at the beach, hearing the ocean. Who knows, maybe I'll go back someday. Telling my mom, I am at the post office. She lets me know that she will be sending the itinerary of their flight to my email as soon as they book it. As I step out of the car with a small package in hand, my phone chimes and it's Xander. The message simply says, *You failed.* What? No way, how did I fail this? I was so confident. Messaging him back, I tell him I am at the post office and will call him as soon as I finish here. As I stand in a very long line, I run the challenge through my head and can't for the life of me figure out where I went wrong. I'm so lost in thought that I don't even realize that the attendant is calling me until the person behind taps my shoulder. After paying, I make my way back to my car and call Xander.

Xander: Charlie!

Charlie: How did I fail?

Xander: Well, hello to you too.

Charlie: I'm sorry, hello. But really, how did I fail? I used all the items.

Xander: That you did, yes. I expected you to go into detail, I asked you to set up the entire scene, but you just talked about how to use those specific items. You could have taken it anywhere, added more items. I wanted to know how you envision the room.

Charlie: Oh.

Xander: So that's why you failed it. Now on to your punishment. No coffee for three days.

Charlie: Really? Well, to be honest, you could have explained this challenge a little better.

Xander: You want seven days?

Charlie: No!

Xander: Then I'd recommend you lose the attitude.

Charlie: I'm sorry. Alright, no coffee for three days then.

Xander: Thank you.

Charlie: You're welcome.

Well, great. Second punishment. Most people would say I got off easy, but to me, this will be a challenge for sure. I drink about three cups a day, and the thought of not having any really sucks. Looking back, I completed that challenge a little too fast. I was overly confident and, in a way, half-assed it. Well, this will definitely teach me.

Day one, no coffee. Instinctively, I started my coffee maker this morning and halfway through realized that I can't have any. I suppose my sink can enjoy it for me. Just as I sit down for lunch, my phone rings with Xander's name flashing on the screen.

Charlie: Hello, Xander.

Xander: Hey, babe. How are you holding up?

Charlie: It's tough, but I will see it through.

Xander: Determination and discipline. That's what I love to hear. Are you eating?

Charlie: I just made a sandwich, nothing special. Are you on your lunch break too?

Xander: I am. As I was sitting here this morning, a thought came to my mind. Well, more like a question.

Charlie: What is it?

Xander: So far, with what we've talked about, do you have any fears?

Charlie: Let me think.

Xander: Of course, take your time. You can al-

Charlie: I do.

Xander: All right, please share them with me.

Charlie: How bad can it get? I mean, how painful?

Xander: You determine that. I will never force you to do more than you can take. Like I said before, it's a slow process, step by step. Once things get physical, we will start out with, let's say, a slap on the ass. It may seem like nothing, but it's the beginning, a very important step.

Charlie: What was your last sub's name?

Xander: Melany.

Charlie: How long were you together?

Xander: About five years.

Charlie: And she was an experienced sub?

Xander: She was.

Charlie: What was the most extreme thing she allowed?

Xander: You really want to know?

Charlie: Yes, I do.

Xander: Ok. She enjoyed the caning stick, a lot. She would want to be caned until she bled.

Charlie: Wow. I can't even imagine that. How could that have been pleasurable for her?

Xander: She said it felt like an outer body experience, and the thought of me causing her to bleed turned her on.

Charlie: That is crazy to me.

Xander: I can understand that. I had a hard time with it at first.

Charlie: Did you enjoy it later?

Xander: Sure, I did. Mainly, her reaction and giving me her trust.

Charlie: What if I can't deliver?

Xander: What do you mean?

Charlie: I mean, what if I figure out that I can't keep up or won't be able to please you in that way, would that be the end of you and me?

Xander: No! First of all, I'm not looking for you to mimic any of my subs. Everyone has their own preferences, their own kinks. I'm simply helping you to find yours. Second, and very important, never force yourself to do something you aren't comfortable with. Third, don't agree to something just because you think it may please me.

Charlie: But after all these years and all of your experiences, I'm sure you have things that you love to do. What if I can't do those?

Xander: We will find a solution together. This isn't Pass/Fail Charlie. There are many grey areas. We will work it out. The word compromise comes to mind.

Day two, no coffee. I'm definitely irritable. I've replaced my morning coffee with a smoothie, but it just isn't the same, probably healthier, though. Today's task is putting on my sexiest dress, taking a picture in a mirror, and send it to Xander, along with a seductive story. This will be interesting, for sure. I'm supposed to meet some of my colleagues for coffee in a little while, and there is no way I can wear the dress I have in mind there. They would look at me like I'm completely insane. Well, I still have about thirty minutes before I have to leave, so I may as well take the picture now. Grabbing the dress out of my closet, I lay it on my bed as I undress. Damn, I forgot just how tight it is as I pull it up my body, but once I have it on, I remember exactly why I love this dress. It's black and comes to about mid-thigh, a halter top that ties around my neck and a section that is cut out between my breasts, leaving just enough for the imagination. I'm sure he won't be expecting me to wear something like this. Braiding my hair down the side, I use a black rubber band at the end and put on my black high heels. When I say high heels, I mean high heels... I can barely walk. Probably why I never wear them. They do make my legs look amazing, though. I accessorize with a few bracelets and a pair of dangling earrings. I've learned to use my imagination when it comes to Xander, complete the scene in a sense. Standing there, staring at my reflection, I try about a dozen different poses until I settle with a hand on my hip and a sweet smile. Yes, it was supposed to be sexy, but I don't want to overdo it or have it come across unnatural. Changing into something more appropriate for a coffee shop, I grab my purse, keys, and sunglasses before leaving my apartment.

Once I arrive, it only takes about two minutes for everyone to show up. As we go inside, we notice it's not busy at all and walk right up to the barista. Three of my coworkers order their coffee's while I still look over the menu.

"Going with something new?" Colin asks, knowing about my usual go-to drink.

"I believe so," I say, playing it off like it's my decision. "Alright, I will go with a small iced green tea."

"You feeling ok?" Maria asks, stopping mid-conversation with Ben.

"Why? Just wanted to change it up," I reply.

"Says the woman who you can't talk to before her morning coffee," Maria snickers.

"Well, maybe I want to cut down on my coffee intake," I reply, and Ben rolls his eyes.

Wow, I had no idea that they saw me as such a coffee addict. This punishment may be a good thing. I'd be happy cutting down to one cup a day, morning, of course. As I sit, lost in conversation with the three, my phone chimes, and I pull it out of my purse.

Charlie,

Just checking in. Staying strong sitting at the coffee shop?

Xander

Ha-ha, very funny Xander

Xander,

I'd make you proud. I ordered an iced green tea.

Charlie

That should make him smile, but really, I want him to be proud of me. Deep down, I believe I may enjoy this punishment just a little.

Charlie,

Well, to each their own. I would have probably chosen something different. How is the task coming along?

Xander

Wonder what he would have ordered?

Xander,

Pretty good. Half of the challenge is complete. Will finish once I get home.

Charlie

And send. Right at that time, Ben asks if I've met someone special because of the permanent smile that's on my lips. Obviously, I'm not going to go into detail about who I am seeing, it's no one's business but my own, so I answer with a simple yes. My phone chimes again, and I check the message.

Charlie,

Sounds good. Enjoy your time with your colleagues. I can't wait to read and see it.

Xander.

When Xander said he would be checking in on me quite often, he wasn't kidding, but honestly, I like it. It's nice to have someone thinking of me, wondering how my day is going and what I'm up to. As soon as I get home, I grab my laptop to complete my task. While sitting in the coffee shop, it hit me, and I hope I can write it down exactly how this scene played out in my head. I begin the message, attaching the picture as well.

Xander,

One evening, you and I decide to go to a club, separately. You get there before me and sit at the bar as I come walking in, wearing the black dress you see in the picture. I look in your direction, and our eyes meet, but I take a seat at the opposite end and order my drink. Never removing my eyes from you, I run my finger over my bottom lip, biting on it slightly before smiling. I move my braid behind me, giving you a glimpse of my neck, veins pulsating. The bartender serves my drink, and I remove the cherry, putting it into my mouth, pulling the stem with my fingers. I notice I have your full attention and use the stem, running it down my neck, biting my lip. One more little smile before I engage in conversation with the handsome young man sitting next to me. You see me giggle and laugh, but I make sure to keep up the silent conversation with you as well. About five minutes later, I get up, walking in your direction, stopping right behind you, placing a note next to your hand before I continue walking. You open the note which says, meet me in the bathroom.

There you go, Xander, what's your next move?

Charlie

Chapter 16

Charlie

5 pm on the dot. In some ways, Xander is very predictable.

Charlie: Hey Xander, how was work?

Xander: Exhausting, actually. My computer kept freezing up, and I ended up losing a few things I was working on.

Charlie: Oh, from your book?

Xander: Yes. Was trying to kill two birds with one stone. No big deal though, nothing I can't rewrite. So, let's talk about your task.

Charlie: You don't waste time.

Xander: Every second spent with you is precious, so no, I don't waste time. Holy hell, I never imagined that coming from you.

Charlie: Too much?

Xander: Not at all. I was blown away. Now I have a question.

Charlie: Ok, what's your question.

Xander: Can you see yourself doing this, or was this strictly made up for the task.

Charlie: The idea came because of you giving me the task. As I was writing it, I really felt myself get into it, though, and it's something I think I would love to try one day. The whole pretending to be strangers' thing. I'm not sure about the bathroom thing, though.

Xander: What exactly do you see happening in that bathroom?

Charlie: Umm...

Xander: Come on, babe, don't get shy on me now.

Charlie: We would probably end up fucking in a stall.

Xander: I love it. You know what you just did there?

Charlie: No, what?

Xander: You revealed a dark fantasy. I knew you had it in you.

Charlie: Oh my god, I did, didn't I? Didn't even realize it.

Xander: I know. Can I give you some advice?

Charlie: Yes?

Xander: Don't overthink things. Let it come naturally and stay true to yourself. Look at what you accomplished, a major step, you should be proud.

Charlie: I think you're right. I really had fun with this one, and once I started writing, it just flowed.

Xander: As it should be. Oh, and by the way, you in that dress, my god.

Charlie: Ah, so you liked what you saw?

Xander: Uh-huh. Amazing. I have another challenge coming your way.

Charlie: Oh, boy, what is it?

Xander: You'll know tomorrow.

Charlie: Don't care to share? Maybe a hint?

Xander: Anticipation, my love. Besides, it's nothing I will tell you over the phone.

Charlie: Oh gosh, what could it be?

Xander: Well, you have about 24 hours to think about it, give or take. Depends when your mail arrives.

Charlie: Mail?

Xander: Yup.

Charlie: You sent me something?

Xander: Yes, your challenge.

Charlie: Now, I'm scared.

Xander: Don't be. It's an easy challenge, too easy actually.

Ok, so he sent me something, and it's coming in the mail. My mind is running haywire, trying to figure out what it could be. Well, it could literally be anything, so it's impossible to figure out without hints. I suppose I'll just have to be patient; it's just a day anyway. I do have a small confession to make. I am falling in love with him, but for some reason, I don't think this is the kind of relationship where we say I love you... at least not yet. He explained that everything will take its time, and nothing is rushed. In a way, I love that. I really get to know him. Hell, to be honest, I feel as if I know more about him than all of my Exes combined. I do have a burning question about vetting time, and since he told me not to hold back, I'll just send him a message now.

Xander,

Hey, I have a question. How long is vetting time?

Charlie

Going into the kitchen and setting my phone on the counter, I grab the ground beef out of the refrigerator so I can get started on the spaghetti. As I put the pot of water on the stove, my phone chimes.

Charlie,

How long is vetting time? You think you're ready for the next step?

Xander

Hell no, I'm not, or am I? Nope, I'm not.

Xander,

No, definitely not. I was just curious. Obviously, you've done this once or twice before.

Charlie

Or three.

Charlie,

Well, it depends on the relationship. Once it took fifteen months, another time nine months, it varies. Is there something else you're wondering about? I feel like you're holding back.

Xander

Damn him, how does he know? There is something I'm very curious about, but would it be too direct? I don't want to come across as desperate or lusting over him. Well, why the hell not? The fact is, I am lusting over him. He reads me like a book anyway, so it's not like it would be a surprise.

Xander,

Ok. I don't want to come across as forward, but when does sex come into play? Is it after the vetting time? Once you know, I'm up for all of this?

Charlie

Ok, writing it out wasn't as hard as I thought.

Charlie,

No, before, and just so you know, we won't be using tools, and I won't be caning you or anything. It will be very natural, and even though I'm not into vanilla, it will be vanilla. When it happens, it is up to us, and there are no set rules. It's when we are comfortable to take that step.

Xander

When we are comfortable to take the next step? How about now?

Xander,

I really love that.

Charlie

I'll leave it at that.

Charlie,

Just so you know, once we get to that level, it won't just be about sex after. It's more like a perk; we will continue working on our bond because that is the most important thing. There could be times we see one another, and we just take a walk in the park and talk. Like I said, this is a very different relationship from what you're probably used to.

Xander

What girl wouldn't want to hear that? Now I kind of wish I had discovered this lifestyle before.

Xander,

That is very different from other relationships I've had.

Charlie

Seriously, I feel as if I hit the jackpot.

Charlie,

I'm glad you actually brought it up. Are you on any type of birth control?

Xander

Wow, of all of the things we've talked about, and this never came up in the past.

Xander,

I am. I had an implant put into my arm about two years ago. It's effective for four years.

Charlie

Best decision ever. I hated taking birth control pills, mainly because it would slip my mind. The procedure wasn't even that bad either. I remember Leah came with me because she thought about one as well, but ended up backing out. I'd do it again in a heartbeat, no questions asked.

Charlie,

Great. That brings me to my next point. I would like for both of us to get tested for sexually transmitted diseases. Safety is paramount.

Xander

I reply, telling him that I think it's a great idea. The timing couldn't be any better; I have an appointment scheduled for my annual next week. I will just ask my doctor to run the tests while I'm there.

Xander

She definitely passed that task. I think I will have that picture of her in that dress in my head for a very long time. Indirectly I got her to reveal a fantasy, which by the way, is something I would love to fulfill in the future. Maybe indirect is the way that is most comfortable for her. I can work with it until she breaks out of that shell. I suppose I will be calling my Doc to see about an appointment for testing. I'm sure he will get me in quickly, I never have to wait too long. This is something I do with anyone I'm involved with, in my view, it's responsible.

I was happy to find out that she is on birth control though, it definitely eliminates the need to wear a condom as long as everything comes back negative. I'm not a fan of condoms, especially during a scene and with the way I play. Hell, I go through several in one night.

The next day I call my doctor's office, and just as I assumed, I don't have to wait long. They scheduled me for an appointment this afternoon at 3 pm.

Charlie,

Hey gorgeous. I have an appointment to get tested this afternoon. Will call you when I get home.

Xander

Looking at the time, I'm sure she is in the middle of teaching her class right now. I get up from my desk and walk into the kitchen, grabbing some lemonade out of the refrigerator. Opening up the pantry door, I debate if I should grab a bag of chips or a banana off the counter.

Chips it is, I went for a morning run today, so I'll see this as my treat. Overall, I live very healthy and make sure I exercise at least five times a week, another form of discipline for me. About twenty minutes later, my phone buzzes on my desk, and it's a message from Charlie.

Xander,

Wow, that's fast. I have my appointment in a few days. Do you know how long it takes for results to come back?

Charlie

It's been a while since I've been tested, but I can give her a ballpark estimate.

Charlie,

It usually takes about a week give or take. I suppose it depends on the clinic you go to. So excited for your challenge?

Xander

Hell, I'm excited for this one.

Xander,

Well, a little terrified, but I will give my best.

Charlie

Always a little negativity in her answer, well, that's Charlie. It's almost as if she uses it as a little safety net, just in case. One day she will leave that net behind, I will get her there. I'm sure she hasn't realized that she is slowly changing, but I've definitely picked up on it. I love it.

Chapter 17

Charlie

I'm practically stalking the mailman right now, waiting on
this so-called surprise package from Xander containing my
challenge. A part of me is a little apprehensive, but then
again, he wouldn't do anything to hurt me. Who knows, he
said it's something I should be able to accomplish easily.
Since I will be coming off of my coffee punishment
tomorrow, the last thing I want is to add more days onto it.
Then it happens, the doorbell rings, and my fingers are
crossed that it doesn't happen to be Leah stropping by. After
opening my door, relief washes over me when I see the
mailman, asking me to sign for a package. I don't even think
my signature is legible, but he didn't care. Shutting my door
and locking it, I carry the box to the dining table and set it
down. Grabbing the box cutter from a drawer, I cut along
the taped seams and take a deep breath. Opening the flaps, I
am met by a ton of red tissue paper, and once removed, I
see a beautiful corset inside. It's very simple, plain black, but
with detailed embroidery. Picking it up, I notice something
else underneath it. A leather blindfold and a red envelope
with my name on it. Picking up the envelope, I carefully
open it, revealing a small note inside.

Challenge:

*I want you to wear this corset, along with the blindfold, and
use your phone to take a picture of yourself, frontal. In the
picture, I want to see you kneeling in anticipation, waiting for
me, hair up in a bun. Use the timer on the camera app.*

Bonus points if you happen to wear black heels. You have until 9 pm today. Thank you.

Xander

I re-read that note about a dozen times, running my hand over his writing, knowing his pen, and hand touched this paper. I swear I'm not creepy or anything, but there is something about it. I close my eyes, and it is at that moment, I long for his touch, even if it's just him holding my hand. This challenge seems very straightforward, and to most, it probably is, but not for me. In any case, I will give this my best shot. Walking into my bedroom with the items in hand, I remove all of my clothing and put on the corset. Just as I thought, it looks beautiful. Walking into my closet, I collect my high heel pumps and put them on. Looking through my underwear drawer, I grab a black pair of lace panties and put them on. Now I stand to face myself in front of the mirror and sigh. How will I take this picture? All I see is a very large, nasty scar running from the top of my breast, down in the direction of my nipple, reminding me of the accident I was in when I was a teenager. So many stitches, it's one of the reasons I never wear low cut shirts. Then my eyes go a bit lower to my hips to the fat deposits that I swore I would get rid of by summer. Well, that didn't happen, obviously. I don't want to fail this challenge, but I don't want Xander to see me this way either. I'm being delusional. With our relationship, he is bound to see all of me one day, but not today, I'm not ready. I chuckle to myself because here I am asking him about sex, but the thought of him seeing me exposed, terrifies me. Then a thought hits me, I can position myself in a way that my scar isn't noticeable, and if I turn a certain way, I'm sure I can catch an angle that will complement those pesky ten pounds I want to lose. Alright, time to get to work.

Twenty minutes go by, and I am ready to just give up. I haven't even gotten to the blindfold part. I hate every single picture I've taken. His instructions say to kneel, why can't I be standing? I know I could get a good shot that way, heck, I already did, figured it was worth a try. That is not the challenge, though. Looking through my camera roll, forty-three pictures, and not one that will work. Either you see my scar or my fat, or even worse, both. Now I am feeling so self-conscious, thinking I will never be able to take my clothes off in front of him. What should I say? I know I will not send any of these pictures, and I honestly don't want to get into the reasons why not, mainly because I don't want to relive the past. I feel defeated, I know I still have over three hours left for the challenge, but it will just be a waste of time. Grabbing my phone, I decide to text Xander, telling him that I failed.

Xander,

I got your package, and first, thank you so much for that beautiful surprise. I regret to tell you that I cannot carry out this challenge, and even though I still have hours left, I'd rather be honest and tell you that this is one I will fail. I accept the punishment.

Charlie

Seconds later, my phone rings.

Xander: What's wrong, Charlie?

Charlie: I just can't do this challenge.

Xander: Why not?

Charlie: I don't feel comfortable.

Xander: I'm not asking for a nude. We agreed on pictures, tell me what is troubling you.

Charlie: You're right, I did agree, and I really tried, I just can't do it.

Xander: I will understand better if you tell me why.

Charlie: Xander, please.

Xander: Honesty, Charlie.

Charlie: Give me time.

Xander: *inhales deeply*

Charlie: *sighs*

Xander: You still have time. Sit down and just think about it. I'm not sure where this fear is coming from, and if you tell me, I can help you, or at least attempt to.

Charlie: I can't right now.

Xander: All right. Are you ready for the punishment then?

Charlie: Yes.

Xander: I want you to edge three times a day for five days. Starting tomorrow.

Charlie: Edge?

Xander: Masturbate to the point where you are about to release and then abruptly stop. Hand only.

Charlie: Orgasm denial.

Xander: Yes. Before you begin, you will message me to let me know. When you finish, you will let me know as well.

Charlie: What? Really?

Xander: Yes, be happy that I won't make you call me while you do it.

Charlie: Oh, my god.

Xander: That's right. I won't expect you to do that, but only because I have a suspicion that you really tried, and something is keeping you from letting go.

Charlie: Thank you, Xander.

Xander: You're welcome, Charlie.

Hanging up the phone, I take a deep breath and lay back on my bed, still wearing this corset. Well, I feel as if I really dodged a bullet here, I thought he was going to deny me coffee for a month. This shouldn't be that difficult. The letting him know beforehand is a little strange to me, but hey, I got off easy. Luckily, I am still off from work so that I can easily accomplish this punishment. I'm thinking when I wake up sometime in the afternoon and then right before bed. Wow, that will be the most I've ever masturbated, I may be sore by the end of each day.

The sun coming through the blinds wakes me, and I grab my phone off the nightstand to check the time. As usual, there is a message from Xander, telling me good morning, just today he added DAY ONE into it. Smartass. Well, I suppose now is as good a time as any to start. No one said punishments are supposed to be fun. Messaging him that I am going to edge, he sends me back a smiley face with the words, ENJOY. Well, it wasn't as awkward as I thought, I suppose we are quite comfortable with one another. Re-reading the word ENJOY, I imagine it coming from his lips. The way the left side of his lip curls up into a little smirk...

something that makes me weak. Closing my eyes, I see him standing at the end of my bed, hands on the metal footboard. His grip is hard. His eyes focused on me like an animal that has been stalking its prey. He lets go and walks up next to me, running his fingertips down my cheek, continuing down my arm, whispering the word EDGE. I take a deep breath, and my right hand navigates underneath my shirt, finding my already erect nipple, running my fingertip over it, sending tingles through me. Biting my lip, I squeeze my breast, and my other hand travels down toward my already moistened panties, slipping underneath the waistband. As I touch the hood of my clit, I can tell that it won't take long before I'm sent into ecstasy, and I will have to be disciplined enough to stop myself before I reach my peak.

Spreading my legs open wide, I start to massage my already oversensitive clit, moving in circles, slowly, so I have complete control. My other hand travels to my other breast, tugging on my nipple, imagining Xander's teeth. I let out a moan, startling myself. I'm never vocal when I masturbate, why now? Even though it's new to me, it heightens the sensation, and I arch my back, moving my fingers faster and faster, feeling as if a spark has ignited that will soon produce a fire that will be hard to tame. My breathing has increased, and I feel myself get close, too close. In that moment, Xander's voice is in my head, saying DON'T COME. I fight my fingers and manage to stop, clenching my jaw tightly. Without a doubt, I know that as soon as my fingers continue, it will be mere seconds until I find release, so my hand moves down further, spreading my folds and inserting two fingers, soaking them completely. Moving them deep inside of me, another moan escapes my lips, and within seconds I've found a rhythm of movement that feels like torturous pleasure. My hand slips out from underneath my shirt, gripping the sheet next to me, almost pulling it off the corner. I have to stop; I have to stop...fuck!

Retracting my hand, I lay it on the inside of my thigh, and a bead of juice runs down my leg. I open my eyes and catch my breath. If anyone were looking in on this, I'm sure they would think I'm insane, letting someone dictate what I do with my body. To tell the truth, I myself would have been one of those people not too long ago, but now I see things differently. I chose to experience this lifestyle, experience Xander. I now understand the reason for the punishment, and I do not want to disappoint him. The challenges and tasks are meant to make me grow, to make us grow together. This is a bond built on trust and honesty, a bond that most people will never get to experience in their lives. Exhaling deeply, I reach for my phone, letting Xander know that I'm through, and just as I predicted, my phone rings.

Xander: How do you feel?

Charlie: Deprived.

Xander: Good. That is exactly how you made me feel by not completing the challenge.

Charlie: I feel that I did learn something, though.

Xander: Please enlighten me.

Charlie: It's all about the bond, the trust. You are helping me grow, push boundaries. Boundaries I want to discover.

Xander: Yes, I wouldn't ask anything of you that I know you couldn't accomplish.

Charlie: I know that.

Xander: Of course, we will hit roadblocks, like the one with the photo. Talking about it will break down those walls and also help me understand. I won't push you on this for now, because clearly there is something that has a hold on you.

Charlie: Yes, I will work on it.

Xander: No, my love, we will work together.

Xander

As I lay in bed tonight, I start going through my daily discipline review of the day. Overall, I'm pleased, except for what happened with Charlie. Was I too harsh on her failing the corset task? Too strict? I think I was disappointed that she was so adamant about not completing it. I still don't understand the issue; it's a very easy task.

Turning around in my bed, I face the window, looking into the night sky. There is supposed to be a full moon, but I don't see it, just a few stars. Then a thought hits me. She didn't do anything wrong. I didn't get her comfortable enough to complete it. I am supposed to give her strength and a level of comfort so she can pass any task or challenge I give her. What was I thinking? Well, what's done is done, but I definitely learned from this.

Jumping out of bed, I run to my desk, grabbing a pen and paper writing myself a note.

Give her strength

Comfort her

Boost her self-esteem

Pinning it on the refrigerator, I stand back, reading it again, feeling confident that I will give all this to her in the future.

Chapter 18

Charlie

I have never felt this deprived in my entire life! I just
finished my last edging session, and I pray that this isn't one
of Xander's favorite punishments. Messaging him after I
finished, nine times out of ten, resulted in a phone call, and
I could just tell he was enjoying the hell out of it on the other
side. After sending today's message, I don't receive a reply,
but I remember him telling me he would be very busy most
of the evening. I get up and start sorting through a stack of
mail I've been avoiding all week. While standing at the
dining table, the storm inside me is growing larger and
larger, and I know it won't take long for me to find release. I
know I'm not supposed to touch myself without his
permission but he's not available to ask, and who knows
when I'll hear back from him. Come on, Charlie, you talk all
day long, you know it's only a matter of time before he calls.
I decide to sit down and watch TV for a bit. Flipping
through the channels, it seems like either everyone is making
out or in the middle of a sex scene. God damn, the agony!
You know what? Fuck it! He doesn't have to know. Lying
back on the sofa, my hand slips into my shorts, and as soon
as my finger touches my clit, that familiar fire shoots through
me, just this time, I get to extinguish it. Opening my legs,
one rests on the coffee table as I start to move my fingers in
haste. I've had days of buildup; this really just needs to
happen right now. It only takes about a minute until I feel
my orgasm approach, and the second it hits me, I start to
scream, my leg knocking over the glass of water and who
knows what else, off the table. With my head back in the

pillow, I try to catch my breath, a feeling a bliss running through me. A second later, my phone rings, fuck, it's him!

Charlie: Hey babe.

Xander: Hey Charlie, sorry it took so long to get back to you.

Charlie: Oh, no problem at all, you said you may be busy.

Xander: Yes...you sound unusually chipper.

Charlie: Me? No, what are you talking about?

Xander: This is not how you sound after edging. You're usually frustrated and whiny.

Charlie: Umm...

Xander: Oh my god.

Charlie: What is it?

Xander: You came without permission, didn't you?

Charlie: What?

Xander: You heard me. Answer the question, Charlie.

Charlie: *sigh*

Xander: I knew it.

Charlie: I'm sorry.

Xander: You will be.

Charlie: Are you going to make me edge for another five days? Please don't.

Xander: Oh no, my love, you have now qualified for two weeks without coffee.

Charlie: You're fucking with me, right? Two weeks?

Xander: I can make it four.

Charlie: No! Please don't.

Xander: Two weeks then.

Charlie: Oh my god, my parents will be here in a week. They are going to think something is up if I don't have coffee with them.

Xander: Well, my dear, you have an imagination. I'm sure you'll come up with something clever.

Charlie: *sigh*

Xander: Thank you.

Charlie: You're welcome.

After we hang up, I toss my phone to the side and close my eyes. Why did I do this? It's not even about the coffee, well maybe a little bit, but more that I broke a rule. I feel terrible for doing it now. It was selfish, very selfish. I know Xander must have been disappointed, even if he came across very cool. Right about now, I have one thought running through my mind, why the hell didn't I just take that stupid picture?

That night, I toss and turn and can't find sleep. Xander called me before he went to bed and wished me a good night, but I am having everything but a good night. Grabbing my phone off my nightstand, I open my chat window and click Xander's name.

Xander,

I hope I don't wake you. I can't sleep because my thoughts are keeping me awake. I broke a rule, and in a way, I'm sure I broke our trust as well. I want you to know that something like this will never happen again. I want you to know that I am taking this very seriously, and I want to be the best I can be.

Charlie

Setting my phone back on the nightstand, I feel much better after getting that out. I just hope I haven't caused too much damage with my actions. The next morning, I wake up to a message from Xander.

Charlie,

I didn't expect to get that message from you. Yes, you broke a rule, but I knew you would. You are learning, and I understand that. I want you to know our trust has not been broken. You also get plus points for telling me this at 3 am.

Xander

Reading his message gives me such a relief, I honestly thought I ruined it. Well, I won't see this as dodging a bullet. I am going to see this as a lesson. When I finally did find sleep last night, I had a bizarre dream. I can't even begin to describe it, but I remember certain things involving being tied up and whipped. I know this had to have been triggered by all of my internet searches involving the lifestyle and maybe also some of the sexy GIFs Xander sends me.

Xander

Charlie, Charlie, Charlie... just racking up those punishments. She's already a week into her no coffee, and I can tell it's getting to her. This is not the typical punishment I give, but I have to work with what I can. I have never been this lenient with any of my other subs, but then again, they were educated subs. Charlie is definitely still a newbie, and sometimes I wonder if she will ever submit to me 100%. I hope she does; I don't want to lose her. I've thought about that possibility and being faced with maybe exiting the lifestyle, but that's not even up for debate. This is who I am; this is who I will always be. On a positive note, our test results came back, and both are all clear. I knew I would be, and I had a suspicion she was as well, but still, you never know. Sitting at my desk, I write down a few ideas that will come into play near the end of the current book I am working on when my phone rings.

Xander: Hey Charlie, how are you?

Charlie: I'm doing all right.

Xander: Caffeine withdrawal?

Charlie: Oh, just a little bit.

Xander: Liar, you're dying a slow death right now, aren't you?

Charlie: I am actually doing ok with it. Who knows, I may give up coffee altogether.

Xander: Uh-huh. I'll believe it when I see it.

Charlie: So, I called because I have a few questions. Is this a good time?

Xander: Of course, go ahead.

Charlie: What is the deal with the collar?

Xander: The deal?

Charlie: I mean, I remember you telling me how you use it. As I did a little research, I noticed pictures of people in clubs wearing them, and I read something about ownership.

Xander: Yes. If you are collared, you are owned.

Charlie: Seriously?

Xander: Yes.

Charlie: So, are you telling me that if we got to that point, I would be wearing a collar all the time?

Xander: No, not all the time. Don't worry; you wouldn't be wearing it while you're teaching kids or when your parents visit.

Charlie: Isn't being owned a little degrading?

Xander: You want to learn about degrading?

Charlie: What do you mean? Is that a thing? Have you ever done that?

Xander: Of course, I have.

Charlie: Can you give me an example?

Xander: All right...let's say you fail to do something I expect of you I would tell you that you are a stupid cumslut, and the only thing you are good for is to be fucked for my entertainment.

Charlie: Oh, my god!

Xander: That's actually pretty tame.

Charlie: Tame...I don't know about tame.

Xander: Well, of course, it's foreign for you, that's why I didn't go any further.

Charlie: You would want to talk to me that way?

Xander: It depends.

Charlie: Depends on what?

Xander: On our relationship and what we agreed upon.

Charlie: Hell no!

Xander: I had a feeling that was coming. Also, getting back to the collar. There are several different ones.

Charlie: Different ones? As in styles and colors?

Xander: Well sure, that too. What I mean are different levels. You start out with a training collar, also called the consideration collar. After that comes the protection collar, known as the relationship collar. Then there is one more.

Charlie: Yes?

Xander: The lifetime collar.

Charlie: Lifetime collar, is that like a wedding ring?

Xander: In a sense, sure. It means so much more, though. If I give you a lifetime collar, I have committed myself to you for life, no matter what.

Charlie: Wow.

Xander: It's very important like I said, means more than a wedding ring to us in the lifestyle.

Charlie: Ok, so here is another question. Since you have this collar thing in the lifestyle, does that mean you don't get married the normal way? Well, the vanilla way?

Xander: No, we still get married the vanilla way, well, not everyone. So basically, you can get married and also have a collaring ceremony.

Charlie: Kind of like two weddings.

Xander: Sure.

Charlie: Well, now since that's cleared up. I know you said that this is the vetting time. What's the next step again?

Xander: Consideration time.

Charlie: What changes during consideration time?

Xander: Well, that's when we take things to the next level. When we put all of the things we talked about and agreed upon into action. We will still continue to talk and grow, that never changes.

Charlie: Ok. Are you any different in this next stage?

Xander: Compared to now?

Charlie: Yes. Like when it really begins, will you still be nice to me?

Xander: I will tell you; I will be firm, rough, strict and demanding. I'm still who I am but definitely stepped up. Since I'm a lifestyle Dom, it's not so much like flipping a switch, but it's different.

Charlie: You've been taking it very easy on me, haven't you?

Xander: Yes, definitely.

Charlie: I may regret this...

Xander: What?

Charlie: I want you to be who you really are with me, like, show me how things will be.

Xander: I can do that. Are you sure you're up for it? I remember you not wanting to take a certain picture for me, and that was an easy task.

Charlie: Yes, I am sure. I don't want to half-ass this, and I don't want to be surprised one day.

Xander: I will always surprise you Charlie, but in a good way.

We ended up talking for another hour, and she definitely had a lot of different questions for me, very good ones too. When she asked what the worst punishment I've ever given was, my answer definitely left her quiet for a moment. Public humiliation isn't for everyone, and I know it's going to make it on her hard limit list eventually. Speaking of lists, maybe I will make that her next challenge.

Chapter 19

Charlie

It's Friday night, and I am waiting for my parents at the airport. The person sitting next to me is enjoying a nice cup of coffee, and the smell is almost driving me insane. Who the hell drinks coffee close to midnight? Better get used to it, my parents drink about six cups a day, each. About five minutes later, I see them walk towards me, and it's then I realize just how much I missed them.

"Charlie," my mom smiles as she squeezes me tight. "It's been too long."

"I know," I reply, my eyes a little bit glassy. "I've missed you."

"Come here, pumpkin," my dad says as he pulls me in after mom releases me.

Once we collect their luggage, we make our way to my car and drive home. It's already super late, and they've had a long trip, so they turn in rather quickly. I only have a one-bedroom apartment, so they are staying in my room while I take over the couch in the living room. My mom said they could get a hotel so they wouldn't displace me, but I told her I wouldn't have it. After getting settled on the couch, I send Xander a good night message before turning out the light on the side table and going to sleep as well.

The next morning, I am awoken by the delicious smell of freshly brewed coffee coming from my kitchen. Great, I am going to fail this punishment; I know I will. Getting up, I

156

walk toward the kitchen and see my mom standing there, preparing breakfast. Damn, I could really get used to this.

"Good morning, mom," I say. "That looks delicious.

"Good morning, honey," my mom replies, giving me a kiss on the cheek. "I have a suspicion that you still don't eat a decent breakfast in the morning. You know I always tell you breakfast is the most important meal of the day."

"I know, mom," I say as I steal a piece of bacon she just took out of the pan. "That's why I bought all this stuff."

"I figured. Would you like a cup of coffee, honey? I brought the one you like," my mom smiles.

"Umm, not this morning mom, thanks. I fell asleep with a headache last night, and it's almost gone," I lie.

"Oh, you should take something," she starts when we hear footsteps coming from down the hall.

"Good morning, everyone," my dad announces as he walks into the room.

I start to set the table for the three of us, and mom brings over the eggs, bacon, toast and, sausage and sets the plates on the table. Once everyone gets settled, my dad brings up prayer.

"Charlie, would you like to lead us in prayer?" my mom asks with a warm smile.

"Um, I can't think of one right this second," I confess, and my parents know exactly that I don't keep up with the whole praying before eating thing.

"Father, we thank thee for the night, and for the pleasant morning light. For the rest, food, and loving care, and all that makes the day so fair. Help us do the things we should, to be to others kind and good. In all we do, in all we say. To grow more loving every day. Amen."

"Amen," my mom and I reply in unison.

"So, Charlie," my dad begins. "Have you found a church in the area? We would love to go to Sunday service tomorrow."

"I have not," I say, and I know I am disappointing them again. I wish I could just be honest and tell them I don't believe in any of it.

"Anyway," my mom interjects. "What are we doing today?"

"I was thinking we could go downtown and walk around a little bit. I know you wanted to check out that big library the last time you were here," I offer.

"Oh yes," my dad replies. "The pictures I've seen are beautiful. Yes, let's do that."

Once we finish the cleanup, I go into the bathroom to get ready for the day. It's right in that moment that I realize I forgot to message Xander this morning. It's not a requirement, but it's just something we do. Stepping back out of the bathroom, I quickly grab my phone and disappear back through the door. Clicking the home button, I already have a message waiting for me.

Charlie,

Good morning beautiful. I hope you'll have a great day with the family today. I will miss talking to you.

Xander

Reading that he will miss talking to me brings a small grin to my lips.

Xander,

I will miss you too. We are going downtown here in a bit, may grab lunch while we are out too. Don't work too hard and message me anytime you'd like.

Charlie

Laying my phone on the counter, I jump in the shower, hurrying since I know my parents still want to shower as well. Once I get out, I wrap the towel around me and see I have another message waiting for me.

Charlie,

You can be certain that you WILL hear from me.

Xander

Hmm, he wrote will in all caps. Just reading it makes me feel tingly inside. A simple message but with so much behind it. Maybe this is the beginning of him stepping it up. A part of me is strangely excited, and the other is a little afraid of what's to come.

Xander

Today I am spending my day at the beach. Shawn and Max are joining me as well and brought some beers along. Sitting in the sand and hearing the waves crash against the shore is almost therapeutic, and I could just close my eyes and drift away. Well, if it weren't for the guys sitting here with me.

"So, Max, where's Roxanne today?" Shawn asks, taking a swig of his beer.

"Her son has a baseball game today, and the non-existent dad decided he wants to show up to support him as well," Max replies.

"So, you can't go?" I ask curiously.

"I've had a few run-ins with that motherfucker. Besides, her son adores me, and I'm going to be the bigger guy and not get in between them. Who knows, maybe he will get it together and actually assume a father role, would be nice for Sam."

"True," I reply, looking out at the water, my mind on Charlie.

"Well, I'd like to announce that I've found myself a slut," Shawn says, playfully coughing. "I mean, sub. I found a sub."

"Oh yeah? It's about time," Max laughs.

"I know, but good things come to those who wait. We talked about our likes and dislikes last week and what do you know, she fucking loves to be degraded. I think I may have hit the jackpot with this one," Shawn says, throwing his hands up in the air as if he's a winner. "Speaking of subs, are you on the search Xander? I know it's been a while since you and Melany parted ways."

"I've met someone," I reply, Charlie's smile crossing my mind.

"Oh yeah? Lifestyler as well?" Max asks.

"Actually no," I reply. "She's not in the lifestyle. Well, not yet."

"Damn, you're not talking about that chick you told me about that attended your takeover. To be honest, it would be too much work for me," Shawn laughs.

"I'm not opposed to work, it just has to be the right person," I respond, finishing off my water.

"You think she's the right person?" Max asks.

"Yes," I say immediately. "100%."

"I don't waste my time with those girls man," Shawn says, handing me a beer, but I decline.

"What do you mean?" I ask.

"Well, you know there are so many of these bitches that say they want to experience our ways, but when it comes down to it, they run away crying. Like that chick from Apex," Shawn explains. "They talk the talk but can't walk the walk."

"Charlie is different. She didn't seek me out for one. She also didn't jump in head first. She's taking this seriously and struggles with things. I believe it's genuine."

"When did you start vetting time," Max asks.

"About six weeks ago," I reply, and he raises his eyebrows.

"Well, my friend, you still have a long way to go. Since you're vetting time takes years."

"Shut the fuck up Max," I laugh.

"Well, he has a point, how long was the last one? Ten months or so?" Shawn asks.

"Nine," I reply.

"See, and she was an experienced sub. Now you're adding her inexperience to it as well. You may be looking at maybe at least a year."

"Look at him," Max adds. "It's not going to take a year. If I didn't know better, I'd say he's fallen for her just a bit."

"No, he hasn't, love grows; it's not just there," Shawn replies, and he has a point.

"Well, you're right," I respond. "But there are exceptions."

Most typical **BDSM** relationships don't start out with love. You meet, you see if you're compatible, you talk, you grow, you form a bond and sometimes love will follow. I can't say I loved any of my three prior subs. When I say three, I don't count the girlfriend that introduced me into the lifestyle. She wasn't a sub, just knowledgeable about certain things and willing to experiment. I can't say I was in love with her either, in lust yes, but not in love. I will admit, my feelings for Charlie are very different, very foreign to me. Maybe that's why I find myself so lenient with her at times. I do have a soft spot when it comes to her. I would have never been this way with the others. No way in hell. Well, she did ask me to be less lenient on her, so I actually have an idea right now. Taking my phone out of my back pocket, I send her a message with a task. I can already tell how she will respond. It doesn't take long, either.

Xander,

What the fuck? You're kidding me, right?

Charlie

Inside I am dying with laughter, just how I predicted.

Charlie,

You have until 7 pm tonight. Thank you.

Xander

Chapter 20

Charlie

My eyes are fixated on the screen of my phone as I re-read his words. *You have until 7 pm tonight. Thank you.* Why the hell would he have me order nipple clamps? What is the purpose?

"Ma'am, would you like some more water?" the waitress asks, pulling me out of my daze.

"Sure, thank you so much," I reply, and she tilts the pitcher, filling my glass.

"Charlie, did you get some bad news?" my mom asks while twisting her fork in the pasta.

"No, not at all," I respond, and I can tell she is curious about what is on my phone right now. "It's just a message from a friend of mine, nothing important."

We continue our lunch and my phone buzzes next to me again. Glancing over, the preview shows a link to a website, and the message reads *Order from here.* As my dad tells a story about a couple doing missionary work in Taiwan, all I can think of is the nipple clamps. I still don't understand the reasoning behind it. He won't be asking me for nudes because I've made it very clear that I will not be sending those, and besides, he's said he doesn't care for nudes at least a dozen times.

Since we had lunch at the LEXINGTON MARKET, we hang around for a bit to check out a few of the vendors. As my parents are deciding on what kind of candy to buy, I decide to just order these damn clamps. Opening the website, I type in the word clamps, and the first result looks as good as any other. Move to shopping cart and check out. Pulling out my credit card, I enter the information and hit the submit button. Once complete, I send Xander a message, telling him I completed the task and receive a *Thank you* a few seconds later.

After finishing up at the market, my mom wants to stop by the mall for some shopping, which basically means, we may as well pitch a tent there. I remember shopping with her when I was younger, and we would literally spend all day at the mall. I will admit she is a smart shopper. She knows all the deals and has told me she recently downloaded an app that gives her even more discounts. She recently turned sixty-five and proudly flashes her ID to get that senior discount as well. Maybe I should pay attention and actually learn a thing or two. As we look through some clothes, my dad sits on a nearby bench, scrolling through his phone.

"It's so nice to spend time with you Charlie," my mom begins. "I wish you didn't live so far away."

"Yeah, I know," I reply. "I do love it here, though."

"I'm still surprised you stayed here after the break-up. Your dad was quite upset that he moved you out here and left you months after."

"It was mutual mom, we grew apart," I reply. "Besides, it was a good career move for me. I make more money, and the cost of living is lower than Cali."

"Well, you're right about that. It seems our insurance keeps going up and I'm glad we bought our house when we did.

It's almost not affordable to buy a moderately sized home now."

"Oh yeah, I remember my crappy apartment and all the money I shelled out for it," I laugh.

"I know you're not alone here, and you have your friends. I just wish you would meet a nice young man, you know, one day we would like some grandchildren."

"Mom," I say, rolling my eyes.

"I know, I know. It would just ease my mind knowing you have someone here that loves and takes care of you."

"It will happen when it's supposed to," I respond, and she smiles, giving me a kiss on the cheek.

Xander

I will be honest; I was a bit surprised that Charlie ordered the nipple clamps without a fight. I know she's dying to know why I assigned this task, but I won't share, they will be there soon enough so she will find out then. Max and Shawn left my place about thirty minutes ago, and I'm about to head into the shower. I love the beach but the feeling of sand all over my body, not so much.

Just as the water runs down my body, my thoughts drift to Charlie, and immediately I smirk. I'm picturing her on her knees, looking up at me. Her lips come into my mind, and I can feel my cock harden. Fuck! What I would give to have that mouth on me right now. The vision of her staring up at me with those blue eyes does the trick, and now I am throbbing. I start to stroke myself and imagine grabbing her hair with one hand, with my other on the side of her neck, moving in and out of her mouth slowly, but determined that she will know that I am in control. When I'm through face-fucking her, I guide her up by her neck and pick her up, carrying her to the sofa. Laying her down, I challenge her mouth with long deep kisses before pinning her down by the shoulders, slamming into her, determined to make her legs shake. My right hand moves to her throat, holding it firm but nowhere near choking. I imagine how she would respond, and I would love nothing more than to hear her moan and cry out in pleasure. Feeling myself come close to my release, I pump harder, faster, and moments later, a loud groan echoes in the bathroom as my fist lands against the wall of the shower. God damn it, what is she doing to me? Getting out of the shower, I reach for my towel when I hear my phone chime.

Xander,

Well, bad news. These clamps are on backorder, so it will take about two to three weeks for them to arrive.

Charlie

Damn, backorder.

Charlie,

Don't worry, no rush anyway. So, hey, I meant to ask, how is the coffee thing going with your parents around?

Xander

I have a feeling she's having a hard time, and I'm surprised that she isn't begging me to allow her to have a cup. Maybe I will surprise her.

Xander,

I'm not going to lie, it's tough. My mom even brought the local coffee from my home. The smell just about killed me this morning. I will survive, though I'm confident.

Charlie

As I read the message, I grin. I'm loving her outlook, so positive. Hell, I told myself I wouldn't be lenient anymore, but oh well.

Charlie,

You know what? I will allow you one cup on Monday morning, but just one. I want a picture of it too.

Xander

Let's see what she says.

Xander,

Oh my god, really? I'm so happy, thank you!!!! How did I deserve that?

Charlie

Yup, just like I thought, totally excited.

Charlie,

You completed your task immediately, without complaining. Figured I would throw you a bone.

Xander

Throw her a bone? Wow, that sounded a little juvenile.

Xander,

Oh my god! I love you!!!!!!!

Charlie

Reading that message stopped me in my tracks just a bit. Deep down, I know it was just a figure of speech, or was it?

Chapter 21

Charlie

It's Monday morning, and I just dropped my parents off at the airport. I really enjoyed having them here, even if it was for a short visit. Of course, my dad reiterated how important it is to find a church that I can attend, and my mom agreed, saying I can meet a very nice young man there. Oh boy, if they only knew. Well then again, Xander is a nice man. I'm sure he would win their hearts in an instant. It's what he does behind closed doors that would give them nightmares for the rest of their lives. I can hear it now, *Charlie, why are you letting someone corrupt you in that way? This is a sin; he is a monster!* I think what would shock them even more, is me telling them that I want to be corrupted in this way. While driving, I hit the call button on my steering wheel, and Xander picks up.

Xander: Hey babe.

Charlie: Hey. Oh my god, I've missed your voice.

Xander: Tell me about it. I've missed yours too. Did your parents enjoy the visit?

Charlie: They did. It was really good to see them.

Xander: Did you ever have that cup of coffee?

Charlie: I did this morning right before we left for the airport. Thank you again.

Xander: You're welcome. You do know that I took it easy on you while your parents were there.

Charlie: A little.

Xander: A little? Well, alright, things are about to change a bit.

Charlie: What do you mean?

Xander: Well, you told me you want to experience me, right?

Charlie: Yes.

Xander: That you will.

I'm convinced that I may have felt a tad courageous the other night when I mentioned that. Maybe I had too much wine. Damn, I was completely sober. This is foreign territory, and I am anything but a risktaker. As soon as I pull up to my apartment, my phone chimes, and I know it's from Xander.

Charlie,

As soon as you get home, I want you to grab that wand, lie on your bed, and message me when you've done so.

Xander

Well, he definitely didn't sugarcoat anything there. Walking up the steps, I unlock the door and walk inside, setting my purse on the table. Walking into my bedroom, I grab the wand out of my nightstand, plug it in, and place it back on the stand. Lying back on the bed, I text Xander that I've done as he commanded.

Charlie,

Good girl. What are you wearing? I want details.

Xander

I reply, telling him I am wearing a blue and white summer dress with pink undergarments.

Charlie,

Remove your panties, spread your legs, and turn on the wand.

Xander

Is this really going to be a *step by step how to masturbate guide?* One thing is for sure; I'm not going to ask. That will just land me back in sassy jail. Following his instructions, I message him back.

Charlie,

I want you to turn it on and run it up and down your left thigh, slowly.

Xander

Flipping the switch, I hold it in my right hand, running it up against my thigh, feeling myself fill with excitement.

Charlie.

Using your free hand, expose your clit and use the wand... DON'T COME.

Xander

Oh my god, is he serious? It's going to be impossible not to come. Lightly placing the wand on my clit, I realize quickly that I can't use much more pressure, it's a guaranteed orgasm, meaning I fail. Moving the wand, alternating the position, I start to moan slightly. A few minutes go by without a message, and part of me wonders if he forgot about me. The wand continues sending tingles through my body, and right as I am about to reach my peak, I change the movement again, depriving myself of release. Complete agony, thanks, Xander. Finally, my phone chimes, and I use my left hand to check it, keeping the wand right where it is.

Charlie,

How are you feeling? Do you want to come?

Xander

He has no idea. I'm not great at texting with my left hand, but the word yes isn't too difficult to get out. The timing is perfect, and I feel like I am about to explode.

Charlie,

Turn off the wand. Grab your panties, put them back on, and call me.

Xander

What the fuck? He has to be kidding? This feels like a punishment. No way, I didn't do anything. Turning off the wand, I throw it off my bed in frustration and put on my panties.

Xander: Charlie.

Charlie: Why?

Xander: Why what?

Charlie: Why didn't you let me come? I don't understand.

Xander: Think about it, is there anything you forgot?

Charlie: Nope.

Xander: Really? Think harder.

Charlie: Xander, the only task you gave me was to order those damn clamps, which I did. You even praised me for doing it so quickly that you rewarded me with the...coffee. Fuck!

Xander: Yes?

Charlie: I forgot to send you a picture of my coffee.

Xander: Indeed.

Xander

Well, this may have been just a little harsh, but she did not follow directions. I'm honestly quite surprised she didn't, but this will definitely teach her that attention to detail is very important. I could hear the frustration in her voice, the need to find release. The sound of her longing voice set something off in me, and I thought about letting her come, but under one condition, on the phone, together with me. We've talked about phone sex before, and the one time she attempted it with a prior boyfriend, they ended up laughing and gave up. She said she thought it was just silly and didn't turn her on in the least bit. Well, my dear, you've never experienced me. I know I can get her there, and I know she will enjoy it.

I actually have a day off today, so I am focused on my book. Just a few more chapters to go until I can send it to my publisher. As I sit here, a thought runs through my head. Charlie has about two more weeks before school starts, so I want to see if we can get together again.

Charlie,

I want to see you next weekend. How does your schedule look?

Xander

About two seconds later, I have a reply with the words FREE. Damn, I can even feel the agony in her message, all caps. This does tell me something, though she is following through with what I tell her. Sure, it's easy to just do whatever she wants since I really can't check up on her per se. A smile comes over my face, knowing that she is serious about this.

Charlie,

Let's meet somewhere halfway. We will figure out a place later.

Xander

I wish she lived closer. It would make things a hell of a lot easier. Even though we are in contact all day long, I still can't just grab her hand or kiss her whenever I feel like it. Unfortunately, all of our meetings have been very short as well. Perhaps we should make an entire weekend out of this. I would love to spend more time with her, and I know the feeling is mutual, even if she would love to kill me right now for making her edge again. Hell, she should be happy that I didn't give her a week.

Chapter 22

Charlie

So originally, Xander and I wanted to meet up somewhere in between our locations, but after looking at what was available, he opted to make the trip to Baltimore instead. I am so excited because he will be staying the entire weekend... with me! I've been in cleaning mode all day, making the place look like a five-star hotel. I also bought some new wax melts for my warmer to make my living room smell like lemons. Xander also mentioned that he has a surprise for me. I'm not great with surprises. I usually try anything in my power to get the information out of people, but I don't push him. I just hope it isn't another challenge. I really am enjoying my morning cup of coffee.

Looking at the time on my phone, I notice it's 6 pm, and Xander should be here at any moment. Luckily, he works from home and can manipulate his schedule a little; otherwise, he would get here super late. A few moments later, my doorbell rings and I rush to the front door, quickly checking my makeup in the mirror nearby. Opening the door, I am met by the man who, with one look, has me at his mercy. Immediately I fall into his arms, kissing him, and he squeezes me tight.

"Charlie," he says. "God, I've missed you."

After exchanging about ten more kisses, he picks up his bag, and we walk inside.

"Wow, it smells great in here. What is that?"

"Wax melts, lemon scented," I reply with a smile.

"Wax? I have some ideas when it comes to wax," he grins. "Where can I put this?"

"Oh, let me show you where the bedroom is," I explain, leading him to my room.

Placing his bag next to my dresser, he opens the zipper and pulls out a small long container, handing it to me.

"What's this?"

"For you," he smiles, and I take it from him.

I open the box to find a single violet rose inside, I've never seen anything so beautiful.

"Wow, that is so beautiful, Xander. Thank you so much," I say, hugging him. "That is so sweet of you."

"The color stands for enchantment. It took me a while to find it, but no other would do."

"It means even more now," I say, almost blushing. "Is this my surprise?"

"Oh no," he replies. "Not even close. Are you hungry?"

"I am, what are you in the mood for?"

"Surprise me," he chuckles.

"I suppose this weekend will be full of surprises."

"Oh, you have no idea. It will be eye-opening for sure; I'll tell you that much."

I have the perfect place in mind, a little French bistro about a half a mile away. It's beautiful outside, so we decide to walk, hand in hand, enjoying the closeness. I really feel like I am floating, and part of me still can't believe my luck. Deep down inside, I want nothing more than to say *I love you* but decide to keep it to myself.

In the restaurant, we sit next to one another, lost in conversation. Suddenly, his hand is on my knee, traveling up the inside of my thigh as he stares directly into my eyes. My speech is leaving me, and I can't concentrate on anything but his hand. My heart is pounding uncontrollably, and within seconds I feel a storm brewing inside. He's completely focused on me, a small smile on his lips. Those eyes, so mysterious, just like him. He moves his hand up and slips under the seam of my shorts. My eyes widen, and I pick up my glass of wine, taking a big sip. Looking over at him, he raises one eyebrow before moving his hand further up. Since my shorts are not very loose, he fights with the material, and I, with my coolness. Leaning over, he kisses my neck, and I close my eyes, enjoying the moment. He removes his hand, and there's no way he's getting up any further, and part of me is relieved. I have no idea what I would have done if his hand would have traveled under my panties.

After dessert, we make our way back home, and he comes up with the idea of watching a movie together. Getting changed into yoga pants and a tank top, I make sure to pull it up high enough to disguise my scar. Walking into the living room, Xander comes out of the bathroom wearing pajama bottoms, only pajama bottoms. The sight of his bare chest immediately sends tingles through me. Taking my hand, he leads me to the couch and sits down, pulling me into him, so my back is against his chest. After browsing the selection of movies on the TV, we choose a comedy. About twenty minutes in, I start to wonder why we decided to watch a movie; we've been talking the entire time.

"How is your book coming along?" I ask as he plays with my hair.

"Good, I have about three more chapters to go before I can submit."

"That's great! I can't wait to read it," I say excitedly.

"Well, maybe I'll give you a little preview when you visit me next time."

"Really? You'll read to me?"

"Well, I was going to let you read it, but if you'd like, sure, I'll read to you," he says, kissing the top of my head. "Happy to have your coffee back?"

"Oh yes, I'm hoping not to lose that privilege again," I explain. "At least not too soon."

"So much for kicking the habit," he laughs.

"True," I reply.

"Sounds like you're ready for another challenge," he laughs.

"Oh no, please, no challenge."

"Kneel!"

"What?" I ask.

"Kneel," he repeats, his tone stricter.

"Right here?" I ask.

"Yes."

Hesitant, I get up from the couch, moving the coffee table just a little and kneel on the floor, my back completely straight, hoping I don't look like an idiot. Xander gets up and walks a circle around me, almost as if he is inspecting.

"Are you comfortable like that?"

"It's ok," I reply, already feeling my thighs quiver.

"I will ask you one more time, are you comfortable like that?"

"No."

"Change it. Don't worry about how you look."

I move, so I am now resting on my calves and exhale.

"Straighten out your arms, palms up," he demands. "Don't move; I will be right back."

This must be the surprise he's been talking about. He said it would be eye-opening, and this is definitely something new for me. Within seconds, I feel my arms tremble just a bit, my nerves getting the better of me. He returns, holding a black scarf and lays it across my hands.

"How do you feel?" he asks, his eyes on mine.

"Curious," I confess.

"Good. What am I about to do to you?"

"Blindfold me?" I guess, not sounding entirely sure.

"Are you sure?"

"No," I reply, and he chuckles.

Removing the scarf from my hands, he walks behind me, running a finger over my shoulder. He then grabs both of my wrists, pulling them behind my back, tying them with the scarf. Next, he grabs my tied hands, his free hand moving my hair to the side and kisses my neck. Enjoying his lips, part of me hopes that he doesn't see my ugly scar. Letting out an involuntary sigh, his hand moves onto my shoulder, moving down the strap of my tank top, and right now, I am just thankful that it's not the left side. I feel his hand move down my breast, slipping underneath my top. His fingers run over my nipple, and it hardens to his touch. He teases me as his lips trail a path from my neck to my shoulder, alternating between kisses and bites. My eyes are closed, enjoying the warmth of his mouth when suddenly, his hand grips my hair, pulling my head closer to him. Feeling the warmth of his breath, he whispers.

"You are mine. Never forget that!"

My breathing increases, a rush shoots through me, and hearing him say those words almost sends me over the edge.

"Are you mine, Charlie?" he asks, demanding an answer.

"Yes," I pant.

"Good, you belong to me, only me. Your body is mine to explore and do with what I want."

Kissing my neck very softly, his hands move to the silk on my wrists, untying it and leaving me wanting more.

"Excellent, you passed your challenge," he smiles, holding out his hand, helping me up. "Come with me."

Nodding my head, I get up, and he leads me into the bedroom. Wow, his demeanor was so...different. One thing is for sure; I want to experience him, all of him. Watching him get into my bed, he reaches his hand out to me, and I grab it. Pulling me close to him, he wraps his arms around me and kisses my forehead asking how that experience made me feel.

"Exhilarating."

"That's wonderful. You may think it's a minor step, but like I said, little by little," he explains.

"My heart was racing, it was insane," I say.

"What exactly made it race?" he asks.

"Not knowing what is happening next," I say.

"Were you scared?"

"No," I respond, and he kisses me.

"Good, you have no reason to be scared, I will take care of you, I mean it," Xander replies. "Are you tired?"

"Yes, a little."

"Good night babe," he says, pulling me close.

"Good night Xander," I reply, closing my eyes.

Waking up the next morning, I move my hand to touch Xander, but all I find is an empty spot. Opening my eyes, I look around the room, did I make all this up? Was it just a dream? Then I see his bag on the floor, silly me. Getting up, I walk into the living room and find an already set breakfast table.

"Good morning Charlie, hungry?"

"Did I have all of this in my fridge?" I ask, trying to remember if I bought orange juice recently.

"Hell no, I went to the grocery store. Do you ever eat breakfast?"

"Usually coffee," I confess, and he shakes his head.

"Maybe I should just forbid coffee for the rest of the year, then you will be forced to actually eat something," he grins.

"Oh, please don't!" I plead.

"Well, this morning, you will have fresh orange juice, eggs benedict, fruit and one cup of coffee."

"Yay," I cheer.

"Let me ask you, did you hear anything I just said, besides coffee?"

"Of course," I giggle.

"Liar!"

While eating breakfast together, I look over at him and smile. Having him here just feels...right. Returning a smile, he grabs my hand, holding it tight.

"It was wonderful waking up next to you this morning," he says, kissing my hand.

"Wish I could say the same," I tease. "I woke up to an empty spot next to me. Falling asleep together was amazing, though."

"It was, it felt like it's how it's supposed to be."

"So, was the challenge my surprise?" I ask.

"Oh no, you will find out tonight."

"Gosh, you really keep me in suspense," I reply.

Chapter 23

Charlie

I've lived in Baltimore for quite some time, but I've never been to this part of town. I'm really wondering where he is taking me. Pulling into the parking lot of a club called K, I wonder if we are going dancing.

Getting out of the car, he grabs my hand and grins, leading me around the building. We find a line of about twenty people in front of us. This place must be quite the hangout. How does he know about it?

"What is this place?" I ask quietly.

"You want me to tell you now or do you want to wait until we get inside and see for yourself?"

Well, I suppose I've made it this far, I guess I'll just wait until we get inside. About ten minutes later, we finally get to the front, and once we go through a set of heavy red curtains, a large room comes into view, complete with a bar and ornate sofas. The room is lit with very dim purple lights, and once I take a look at the crowd, I realize where he has brought me.

"Surprised?" he asks with a smile.

"Very! This is a BDSM club, right?"

"Yes, I've never been to this one; it's fairly new," he explains, holding my hand tightly.

Moving through the crowd, he leads me into a room, and the first thing I notice is a fully naked woman tied up to a cross, blindfolded. The Dom has a crop in his hand, running it over her body. My eyes follow the crop as he runs it over her vagina, down her left leg. Watching her body react with pleasure has me fascinated, and it's almost as if I can feel the sensation on my own body, even though I've never experienced it. My eyes peer to the right and widen immediately, a little shocked. I see another woman, tied up to the point where she can't move, lying on the couch, head pushed into the pillow, and a guy fucking her from behind, roughly. I can't believe they are doing this right in front of everyone, and it doesn't seem to bother them who is watching. Instinctively, I move my eyes to the ground, not wanting to stare. I also see people strapped to devices that I have never seen before. What am I saying? All of this is foreign to me. Looking around, I notice that more and more people are having sex around me, filling the room with loud groans and screams. It's amazing how comfortable everyone is and how in tune these couples are with each other.

"What do you think?" Xander asks, moving closer to my ear.

"Wow," I reply, and he leans in, kissing my temple.

"Want to check out another room?"

"Definitely," I respond, curiosity getting the better of me.

In the next room, there are a ton of very large plush seating areas with many pillows. I also notice a lot of mirrors on the walls and a huge pole in the middle of the room. People are definitely making use of this area as well. I've gone from never seeing anyone fuck in front of me to losing count. There is one thing all of these people have in common; everyone is free and having a great time. Xander leads me to a seating area, tucked away in a corner, and we talk, his hand

186

resting on my thigh. About thirty minutes later, a man and woman come up to us and ask if we would like to participate in some couple on couple fun. My eyes must be huge because Xander just shoots me a grin and declines for us. After they walk away, Xander chuckles.

"They were serious?" I ask.

"Of course," he replies.

"They don't even know us," I reply.

"They don't have to, they aren't looking to get married," he jokes.

"Well, I know that, it's just a little strange to me."

"I understand. Sometimes people will come up and ask for threesomes, gang bangs, and many other things," Xander explains, and now I am wondering.

"Have you ever had a threesome?" I ask.

"Many," he replies, stunning me just a bit.

"What kind of threesomes have you had?"

"Usually, it was my sub and another woman. Once in a while, we would bring in another man, but he would just end up fucking her. I don't play with men."

"You didn't have a problem watching your sub get fucked by another guy?" I ask, baffled in a way.

"No, it never really bothered me; it was something we agreed upon beforehand," he explains.

"Aren't there feeling involved, though?"

"Remember when you asked me if I ever was in love?"

"Yes," I reply. "You said you haven't been."

"That's why," he responds. "I think if I loved them, it would be different."

"Have you had gang bangs?"

"Yes," he admits, and I take a deep breath.

"I assume you've also done couple on couple," I say, and he nods.

"Do you see me in a different light now?" he asks.

"No, of course not. It's just quite a bit to take in; everything is very new. Just so you know, I am not and won't be into any of that."

"That is completely fine," he says, wrapping his arm around me and pulling me in for a kiss.

"You don't think you will miss that?"

"No," he replies. "I am looking forward to what we will share together."

As we make our way to the last room, I see that it is quite a popular one. Xander informs me that this is the suspension room, and it wears its name well. I see chains hanging from the ceiling and rope on the walls. I see a man, who I assume is a male sub, tied up with god knows how much rope, hanging freely in the air as a female writes words all over his body. I can make out the word's *ass for fucking* and *fuck slave,* and I quickly realize that she is degrading him. I know everyone has their own kink, but this is one I do not understand. Once we get back into the lounge, we notice it has cleared out just a bit, so Xander loosens his grip on my hand. A few minutes later, we are approached by a man that

Xander knows, and the three of us engage in conversation. Suddenly I feel someone grip my waist, pulling me toward them, and fear immediately grips me. Not a second later, Xander grabs my arm, pulling me behind him.

"What are you doing?" Xander says, demanding an answer from the man.

"I'm going to teach that bitch how to be a good sub," the man responds, obviously quite tipsy.

Immediately Xander grabs the man by the arms, pinning him to the wall, staring him directly in the eye.

"You are not touching my woman," Xander growls.

The man tries to free himself from Xander's grip, really struggling.

"If she were your bitch why isn't she collared, you idiot?" he yells.

I can feel my entire body shake, the way this man just assumed he could take me as if I were some item on a shelf. Everyone else we've encountered has been very polite and respectful; I really hope this isn't the norm.

"How about we talk to the dungeon master, and he will make a decision about your disrespectful behavior," Xander replies, letting go of the man's arms.

Since this caused quite the commotion, the dungeon master appears, and the situation is discussed. Apparently, this man has already had a few warnings tonight, and his little stunt with me just got him thrown out of the club. My body may have been shaking a moment ago, but after seeing Xander and how he protected me, it really warmed my heart. This just made me fall for him even harder. As soon as the man is escorted out, Xander takes me in his arms, apologizing for what happened.

"If I ever take you to another club, you will be collared."

Xander

What the hell was I thinking? Of course, this asshole was entirely out of line, but leading her in without a collar was a fucked-up move on my part. No collar equals available; I will never make this mistake again, ever. I can tell she was afraid, and I hated to see her this way. That guy is lucky he didn't end up with a broken nose. We end up leaving the club about twenty minutes later, enough excitement for one night. Right now, I just want to be alone with her, hold her, comfort her. Lying in bed together, I hold her in my arms, wishing we could stay this way forever.

"So, this happened because I wasn't wearing a collar?" Charlie asks, curiously.

"Remember, a collar shows ownership. By you not wearing one technically, it equaled availability, though he should have never behaved the way he did."

"I see," she replies.

"We are not at a point where you would be wearing a collar since this is still the vetting period, but I swear, the next one we visit, you will wear one," I say.

"I'm ok with that," she replies, and I kiss her lips.

"Can I ask you something," I ask, and she nods in agreement. "Why didn't you want to take a picture in that corset?"

For a long moment, there is complete silence in the room, and again, I can tell that there is a reason.

"Charlie, you can tell me anything, you know this," I say, and she takes a deep breath.

"I have a very ugly scar on my right breast that I got from a bad car accident when I was a teenager. When I put on the corset, it was so visible that I just couldn't do it."

"How bad was this accident?" I ask.

"My friend was killed. She was driving, and I was in the passenger seat. I remember waking up in the hospital with a broken arm, leg, cuts, and bruises. When I learned that my friend died, I just wanted to cry but couldn't because of all of the pain I was feeling. I don't even remember what really happened to this day; it's like my mind blocked it out."

"I am so sorry Charlie, a loss like that is tremendous, and I can imagine how much mental and physical pain it caused you," I say, pulling her closer to me.

"Thank you, it's been years, but it still hurts at times."

"Will you show it to me?" I ask.

"My scar?" she asks. "Not yet. I will, but not right now."

"I can respect that," I reply, pulling her closer and kissing the top of her head.

I was right; there was a reason. God, I wish she would have shared this with me at the time, I would have never punished her for that. She needs to know that she is safe with me, that she can tell me everything.

Chapter 24

Charlie

What a weekend. When Xander said it would be eye-opening, he wasn't kidding. Some of the things I've seen definitely left me speechless and others very fascinated. He's only been gone a few hours, and I already miss him terribly. Luckily, I remembered to have him sign Leah's book. She has been pestering me non-stop.

School starts a week from tomorrow, and I'm actually scheduled to work starting Tuesday. It's the same every year, getting the classrooms together, checking rosters and a few meetings. I got an email from the principal just the other day, informing me that I won't have anyone shadowing me. Apparently, the person decided not to take the job. I'm meeting up with the girl's tomorrow night for dinner and drinks, it feels like it's been a while since we've all gotten together, so it's time.

As soon as Xander makes it home, he calls, and we stay on the phone for a few hours. I've gotten pretty good at getting a lot of things accomplished while talking to him. I remember the first few weeks; my laundry was piled up to the point of embarrassment.

Later that night, I lie in bed and think about what a turn my life has taken. Honestly, it's probably nothing compared to what is ahead. I wouldn't trade it for anything, though. I have never had a relationship where my partner and I communicated so much. Even though it's new, I absolutely love it. There is no room for doubt or wonder. Sure, there may be some minor things that aren't discussed but all of the important factors are always laid out on the table. He is the first man that can coax things out of me that I never imagined telling a soul. I suppose that is where trust comes in. He always says that we are working toward making our bond stronger; I believe I finally realize what this bond really is. There are times we look at one another, and no one has to say a word, a silent conversation between minds, simply beautiful.

A few days later, I'm sitting in my classroom, placing the nameplates of the new students on their desk as my phone chimes. Walking toward my desk, I see I have a new email, so I check to see what it is. Well, it looks like the nipple clamps made it here just a few days early anyway; apparently, they have been delivered and are currently in my mailbox. Hopefully, they did make it to my mailbox. Our mailman has a difficult time placing the mail in the right boxes. How embarrassing would that be if my neighbor came knocking on my door holding my package of nipple clamps. Luckily, the website says their packaging is discreet; otherwise, I could imagine the shade of red I would be turning.

After finishing the day with one last meeting, I make my way home, stopping at the grocery store on the way. I don't feel like cooking tonight, so a chef salad sounds perfect. Unlocking my mailbox, I see a white plastic bag with my address printed on it, no return address. Walking up the stairs, I unlock my door and go inside. Immediately, I open the envelope and see the clamps packed in a small clear bag. Shivers run down my spine as I get a flashback of all the GIFs Xander sent me with women wearing them. Whenever he sent one where they were being pulled, I cringed just a bit. Dear God, I hope they don't hurt. Taking them into my bedroom, I open the little plastic flap and let them fall into my hand. They aren't on the light side, and as I inspect them, I notice a third clamp on a long chain. What the hell is that for? Holding them up, it almost looks like a T, and I figure that maybe the other is used to attach it somewhere so that you are tied to something in a sense. Grabbing my phone, I open the website from where I ordered and look at the buying history. OH MY GOD! I ordered nipple clamps that include a clit clamp. Well, this will teach me to read the description next time. Chuckling at my error, I take a closer look, and soon curiosity has the best of me. I wonder what it would feel like...oh hell, let me try it. Getting completely undressed, I grab the clamps, pinching the nipple on my left breast, pulling slightly to attach the clasp. Letting go, I'm surprised to find that it isn't as painful as I assumed. I attach the right side, and now I begin fiddling around with the third. Unsure how to attach it, again, I grab my phone, searching for images. All right, looks easy enough, I'll try my best shot. As soon as my hands leave the clasp, I let out a bloodcurdling scream. Holy fuck! How can anyone stand this? Pressing the springs to remove it, I can't believe just how much more painful that is, so I let go, and I'm back where I started, a clamp attached to me that feels like razors digging into my skin. Taking a deep breath, I bite my lip hard and press again, removing it completely. At this point, I've had it with clamps and remove the nipple ones as well, each with their own level of pain, and toss the chain contraption across the room. I can't imagine this being a turn on for any woman; this was obviously made with the man's perspective in mind. Putting on my bathrobe, I decide to give Xander a call.

Xander: Hey babe, I was just thinking of you.

Charlie: Hey.

Xander: Everything all right? You sound different.

Charlie: Well, the clamps came in today, and I realized I ordered the wrong ones. I ordered the ones with the clit clamp too. I just want to make it very clear that there is no way in hell that you and I will ever use them.

Xander: Oh wow, you went all out. I like it. Well, you can't knock it before you try it.

Charlie: Oh, I did, and that's why I am saying, no way in hell.

Xander: You tried them on?

Charlie: Of course.

Xander: Oh, Charlie.

Charlie: What?

Xander: I have bad news for you.

Charlie: Why bad news?

Xander: You are not to try anything without my permission, ever.

Charlie: Huh? Are you saying I had to wait until you said it was ok?

Xander: Yes.

Charlie: Well, I'm sorry to say, my Dom never informed me of this ridiculous rule.

Xander: *chuckling*

Charlie: What's so funny?

Xander: Your Dom never informed you of this rule?

Charlie: You didn't.

Xander: Think back, I did. I was just about to give you two weeks of no coffee for not asking permission, but because of that attitude and sassiness, you just qualified for three weeks, including one week of edging.

Charlie: Fuck my life.

Xander

Ok, so three weeks of no coffee and a week of edging may have been a little excessive, but she was wrong. I told her in the beginning that if I ever instructed her to order something, she may never use it without my permission. The no coffee will really be a challenge for her now since work just started again, but hey, you have to learn somehow.

Even though I am very disciplined in general, I can't seem to concentrate on my work. I find my thoughts drifting to Charlie, and the weekend we spent together. Some of my favorite moments were holding her in my arms at night, drifting off to sleep. It's a closeness I've been missing since I left, almost like a void. The moment she knelt in front of me, I felt a step closer to our common goal. I was very proud of her, as well. Kneeling may not seem like a big deal but at that moment, she handed power over to me. The smile fades from my lips when I think of that asshole in the club and the way he put his hands on her. That is not at all how her first **BDSM** club experience should have been. That moment did give me another realization. I care for her more than I thought I would, at least in this amount of time. Things were very different with my other subs, more structure, less play. Why the hell am I comparing her? She is nothing like the others, and maybe deep down, she is precisely the kind of woman I crave.

Chapter 25

Charlie

It's been six weeks since Xander's visit, and even though distance and sometimes life comes between, I've never felt closer to him. He had made plans to visit me about three weeks ago, but unfortunately, he had to fly to New York for a last-minute book signing. Apparently, the other author was sick, and the publisher asked if Xander would go in his place. I would have loved to fly there to see him, but I had already promised Brynn that I would watch her dog for the week. At least the signing went very well, he sold all of his books, and they want him to come back for another signing very soon. I remember the happiness in his voice when he called to tell me the news. This was only his second signing, and he said the first one didn't go well. I actually had to convince him to go, the thought of canceling on me didn't sit well with him at all. I am also happy to report that I've survived my punishments and plan to accumulate less in the future.

In our last few phone calls, I've asked Xander about his prior subs, things they did, what they craved. He's like an open book, telling me anything I want to know. I am fascinated by the stories and shocked by them as well. I will admit, once in a while; they do make me just a bit insecure because I'm not sure that I can keep up with them. They were so experienced, so open to... anything basically. I can't imagine getting suspended into the air or tied, naked, outside to a tree while he has his way with me. The club came into my mind a few times as well. Having sex in front of strangers...not sure I could do that either.

Today is Saturday, and I'm thrilled to be off work, I've actually slept in for a change, and it was amazing. Grabbing my phone, I see I already have a message from Xander waiting for me, and instead of replying, I decide to call him.

Xander: Good morning Charlie, did you sleep well?

Charlie: I did, I'm still lying in bed.

Xander: Mmm...well, maybe I should tell you about my dream then.

Charlie: Please do!

Xander: I dreamt you and I were all alone at the beach. While in the water, I lift you up on a large rock, pulling your bikini bottoms aside, tongue fucking you. You throw your head back, moaning, gripping my shoulders while my nails rake down the inside of your thighs.

Charlie: Whoa, that is one hell of a dream.

Xander: It definitely had an effect on me.

Charlie: Are you turned on right now.

Xander: I'm edging.

Charlie: Seriously?

Xander: Yup.

Charlie: I don't even know what to say right now.

Xander: What's on your mind? Just let go, what would you want me to do to you right now if I was there.

Charlie: Um...gosh Xander, this is so awkward.

Xander: Charlie, it's me. Just be natural.

Charlie: I told you I tried this before and it didn't go so well.

Xander: All right. I have a challenge for you.

Charlie: Oh great.

Xander: I love the enthusiasm. Anyway, come up with a scenario and implement dirty talk. You have until 9 pm tonight. I will let you use chat tonight, just want to make sure you're comfortable.

Charlie: I'll give it my best shot.

Xander: That's the spirit.

Dirty talk. I remember trying it with my Ex-boyfriend, and I just felt like a fool, like I was playing some sort of role. At least I have eleven hours, and how bad can it be over chat?

After getting out of the shower, I get a message from Leah saying she's on her way over for a visit. There must be guy trouble that she wants to vent about. She and David didn't' really work out, and I remember her saying she met this older guy, but there were several red flags right from the start. As I dry my hair, my doorbell rings, so I turn off the hairdryer, laying it on the counter. Opening my door, I'm met by Leah.

"Wow, you just texted me, I didn't think you would be this fast," I comment, and she comes inside.

"I was in the area already. Charlie, this fucking loser, I want to kill him," she says, plopping down on the couch.

"What happened?"

"Well, this fucker is actually married and has children," she explains, and my eyes widen, not quite what I was expecting.

"Oh wow," I say, covering my mouth. "How did you find out?"

"I was at the coffee shop waiting on my to-go order, and this idiot comes walking in with his family. For a moment, I just watched him, and he was all sweet to his wife, unbelievable," she huffs.

"I'm so sorry, did you call him later to confront him?" I ask.

"Come on Charlie. I confronted the ass right then and there. His wife was so shocked, and I hope she ends up leaving him."

"You definitely have balls," I say, grabbing a glass of water for each of us.

"If he thought he could just fuck me for fun and go home to his wife, he was messing with the wrong bitch."

"He experienced the wrath of Leah," I say jokingly.

"Oh, he sure did," she chuckles. "Anyway, how are things with Xander?"

"Really good actually, I'm hoping we can meet up soon again. It sucks living in different places," I sigh.

"I'm sure it does. Wish I could find someone like him. He seems like such a nice and normal guy, down to earth. Can you duplicate him, please?"

After laughing about that for a moment, Leah continues telling me about some gossip, and my mind drifts to Xander. I wonder what Leah would say if she actually knew who Xander was or what direction my life is taking. Most people would think I'm off my rocker, but then again, who cares. It's my life, and I can make my own decisions.

The day seems to fly by, and it's already ten minutes until nine. All of my research left me emptyhanded. What the hell am I going to write him? I don't want another punishment; I want to be able to complete this challenge. Then I think of one website I stumbled across. It basically said just imagine yourself with the person and let your fantasies run wild. I've had dreams of Xander before, I've even sat here daydreaming about different things. That's what I'll do; I'll wing it and let's see what happens. I'm going to take it a step further, I'm calling him.

Xander: Hey Charlie, I was expecting a message.

Charlie: I come into your room, eyes on you, slowly walking toward you.

Xander: Oh?

Charlie: As I reach you, I kiss your lips as my hands undo the buttons of your shirt, ripping off the last few. My mouth is on your neck, alternating between kisses and bites while my hands find your belt, undoing the clasp and pulling it out of the loops, tossing it on the ground.

Xander: *Groans*

Charlie: Pushing your pants down your hips, my fingers find the waistband of your boxers, tugging them down as well. Next, I kneel down in front of you, one hand is on your cock, stroking you, while my other hand is on your hip, nails running down.

Xander: God damn it.

Charlie: My tongue touches the head, running circles around it, teasing you.

Xander: Fuck, Charlie!

Charlie: Now you feel my lips around you as I take you in, all of you.

Xander: You are driving me insane.

Charlie: You feel me moan on your cock as I suck you hard, coating you, making a mess.

Xander: My hand grips your hair, pulling you off me and up to your feet. Turning you around, I push you to the wall, and I finger you as I bite your neck.

Charlie: *moans*

Xander: Once you are soaking for me, I slam my cock into you, holding your wrists against the wall.

Charlie: Oh, my god.

Xander: I want you to scream for me. Let go and come for me.

Charlie: Fuck!

Did this really just happen? Not only did we have phone sex, we even came together. Unbelievable. This was over the phone; how intense will it be in person? God, his groans send shivers down my spine, so fucking sexy. We definitely have to do this again. Chuckling to myself, I sit here shaking my head. Typical me, refuse to try something new and then can't get enough.

Chapter 26

Charlie

One month later.

I'm on my way to Ocean City, finally. It's unbelievable that it has taken this long to get together. Every weekend we chose ended up not working out. Last weekend Xander called and told me he had a death in his family and had to fly to Florida for the funeral. Even though he wasn't close to his aunt, I understood that he had to be there. I'm actually happy he was able to see his mom again. He's told me they've always been close and wishes they'd see each other more often. I am really excited to finally see Xander's house, the views I've seen on pictures have been breathtaking. Our conversations have been very interesting, to say the least. Phone sex has become the norm, and even if we are just having a regular conversation, one of us ends up getting turned on. It's kind of cute when it's me, I kind of hint at it, like beating around the bush. When Xander initiates, he pretty much just lays it out. My toys have never been used this much before, but I love it. Most of the time, Xander is strict, precise, and dominant during those calls, but there are times he lets me take control and seems to really enjoy it. While talking yesterday, I asked if he would show me a few of his *'tools'* and he said he would be happy to. Now, I am definitely not anywhere near wanting to have any of them used on me, but I am anxious to see them in person.

I've been stuck in traffic for the last thirty minutes, and I swear there must be an accident up ahead. My thoughts drift to the time he had me kneel in front of him. When I felt his fingers on my skin, a feeling of excitement came over me.

That night I wanted something more to happen, but I was afraid to initiate. Falling asleep next to him was amazing, he's unlike any guy I've ever met.

Wow! Finally, we are moving. According to the app on my phone, I have an hour left until I arrive. Turning up my music, I sing along to the songs I recognize, probably quite badly, but at least I'm on my own. Luckily, good music always makes the time go by, and as I pull up to Xander's driveway, my eyes widen. Damn, I would love to live here. Typical beach house, not too big or fancy, just right. Getting out of my car, I pop the trunk, grab my bag, and make my way to the front door. Ringing the bell, it only takes Xander a few seconds to answer.

"Charlie! I thought you'd never get here," he says, pulling me in and kissing me.

"Yeah, I'm not quite sure what the holdup was. I literally just sat stuck in traffic for about half an hour but never saw evidence of a wreck," I reply.

"I'm just glad that you are here," he says. "Here, let me grab your bag."

Walking in, he grabs my hand and leads me into the living room, and my eyes go to the large windows overlooking the water. This really is a dream; maybe I should come to visit him from now on. My apartment is a joke compared to this.

"Here I'll show you the bedroom; you can unpack if you'd like," Xander offers.

"Is that where you have your tools?" I ask, feeling a little silly.

"I do," he smiles. "You want me to break them out now?"

"Yes," I say, giggling a bit.

Once we step into his bedroom, I'm pleasantly surprised. I honestly thought I would step into a room that mirrored a torture chamber, but there is not even a hint that reveals his lifestyle.

"Wow," I comment.

"What?" he replies.

"This is so...normal."

"What were you expecting?" he asks, raising an eyebrow.

"I don't know," I begin. "I thought you'd have a wall lined with floggers, crops, and whips. I also pictured a not so normal bed."

"Well, my tools are all put away. The bed isn't a normal bed, though. Take a closer look."

I walk over to the four-post bed that is perfectly made, almost too perfect. Placing my hand on the wood post, I slide it down, my eyes investigating.

"Those rings," I say, pointing to the headboard.

"Good job."

"So, that's where you tie people up?" I ask.

"Charlie, the way you say people makes it sound like I have a rotating door here. Yes, it's where I would tie you up," he smiles, and the thought sends tingles through me.

"With rope?"

"Rope, chains, handcuffs, ties. Whatever we agree on," he explains, and I feel his hand on the side of my neck, pulling me in for another kiss. Fuck, just throw me on the bed already, I can't take this. "What do you want me to show you first?"

"How about a flogger?"

Kissing my cheek, he releases the grip on my hand and walks into his closet, returning with a black and blue flogger. Handing it to me, I take it in my right hand, running my fingers through the long soft leather strips. I'm actually loving the feel of it; I can see this being pleasurable if done correctly.

"Do you like it?" he asks, and I nod.

Heading back into the closet, I'm still playing around with the leather strips as he returns, handing me a crop.

"Okay, this looks a little more painful," I say, holding it in my hand, my eyes focused on the tip.

"It depends on how it's used. I can definitely bruise you with it, or just run it down your body to build anticipation."

Giving myself a quick whack on my hand, I definitely feel a sting and close my hand. I already think I am a fan of the running it down my body, but smacking me with it? Not so much. Leaving my side again, he returns with a clear box filled with all kinds of things and gestures for me to have a seat on the bed next to him.

"Alright, here we have handcuffs, blindfold, anal beads, a paddle, nipple clamps," he begins.

"Not using nipple clamps," I protest, and he rolls his eyes.

"We will see, let me place them on you, and you may change your mind."

"This one doesn't have the clit clamp, does it?" I ask.

"No," he laughs. "Though we can always buy that variety, or you can bring yours."

"No, thank you," I say, shaking my head. "I have a question."

"Ask," he smiles, kissing my cheek again.

"So, you've used all of these things on women before?"

"Not these items. Everything is brand new. I would never use anything on you that I used on someone else," he explains, and I'm a bit relieved.

"Pricey hobby you have there," I joke.

"Kind of," he says, scratching the back of his head.

"So, what else do you have in your bag of tricks there?"

"Butt plug," he replies, holding a silver thing with a gem on it.

"What the heck?" I start. "I mean, I obviously can assume where that goes, but why?"

"To me, they are beautiful. It's also an intense feeling for the both of us when you wear one. They are also used in preparation for anal sex."

"Ah," I say, thinking what the fuck have I gotten myself into?

He shows me a few other things and explains what they are and how they are used. I keep going back to this flogger, though; it's cute. I playfully smacked him on the ass with it when he got up to grab something else, and the grin on his face was so adorable.

Xander

I spent most of the day tidying up my place, well, half the day. I don't have much clutter, and I'm very good at not leaving things lying around, well, except for on my desk, that is definitely a mess. Hell, I'm a writer, it's my excuse, and I'm sticking to it. I was a little worried that something happened to Charlie since she was a little late, but traffic can be a bitch sometimes. The moment I saw her standing at my door was a moment I've been waiting for for a long time; actually, the both of us have been waiting for a long time.

I must admit, I love her curiosity. There is something so innocent yet daring about her. The way she was holding and looking at the flogger... I almost wanted to ask if she wanted me to use it on her right then and there. Maybe I should have actually. No, what am I saying? She just arrived, and I have my way of doing things, I'm not going off track, even if my inner demon wants me to. Speaking of my inner demon, it's something I still have to tell her about, something very important actually. Not now though, not this weekend.

"I'm ready," Charlie smiles, walking out of the bathroom, in a little black dress with black heels, god damn!

"You look, gorgeous babe," I comment, walking toward her and grabbing her hand. "Go ahead to the living room, and I'll be right there."

As soon as she leaves the room, I walk into my closet and retrieve a black box that's tied with a ribbon. Quickly, I set it on the counter in the bathroom before shutting off the light to meet Charlie in the living room. Grabbing my wallet and keys, we walk out to my car to go to dinner. I've made reservations at one of my favorite places in town. I actually haven't been there in quite some time; it's not one of those places you go to on your own. It's definitely upper class with a dress code, perfect date night.

After arriving, we are seated immediately, and the waitress pours us each a glass of wine, complimentary service. I'm really happy with the location of our table, tucked away in a corner, dim lights, overlooking the ocean... I couldn't have written it better.

Unfortunately, we are sitting across from one another. I would much rather sit beside her so that simple movements could go unnoticed. Well, I guess I need to be a good boy, at least here. As soon as we get home, though... that's when there will be no holding back. I have to have her.

Chapter 27

Charlie

We just got back to Xander's house, and before unlocking the door, he pulls me into his arms, kissing me with no reserve. Sexual tension has been building all night long, and if he doesn't make a move tonight, I may have to. There is no way I can wait any longer. Can I make a move? I know he's the Dom and basically in charge, does that mean it's all up to him? Then again, we aren't entirely into it yet, just testing the waters, so to say, I think. After releasing me, he grabs the keys out of his pocket, searching for the house key.

"Charlie," he begins as he unlocks the door.

"Yes," I reply.

"I have a challenge for you," he smiles, and I sigh, a challenge was the last thing on my mind, I fucking want him.

"Okay, what is it?"

"I want you to walk into my bathroom. I have a surprise waiting for you there. Come find me after."

"Do I get a hint?" I ask, and he chuckles.

"No need, you'll find out within a minute if you move fast," he says, slapping my ass as we walk in.

Laughing to myself, I walk into his bedroom, my hand brushing the soft comforter on his bed. Kicking off my heels, I place them next to my bag near the dresser and walk into the bathroom. On the counter, I see a large black box wrapped with a red ribbon. After untying the ribbon, I lift up the top and close my eyes, letting out a deep sigh. Fucking corset. What is his fascination with these things? Well, then again, obviously I want to fuck him, it's not like I wouldn't be exposing myself. This may be the time I need to get over myself and embrace my flaws. He knows about my scar and the story that comes along with it. After staring at my reflection in the mirror for about three minutes, I walk toward the bathroom door to shut it before undressing. The corset he sent me was beautiful, but this one wows me. It's black and dark blue. He also included a matching thong... I hate thongs! All right, enough with the negativity. It takes me just a bit to get myself into the corset, and after another deep inhale, I manage to hook the last three clasps. Taking a look at the woman staring back at me, all I can focus on is that long mark covering my breast, which seems to be accentuated by the corset pushing my breasts up. Great, I have the same exact feelings coming back as before. Well, at least he didn't say I had to put my hair up in a bun, or did he? I search the package for a note but come up emptyhanded, thankfully. Taking one last look in the mirror, I look down at my hips, and I'm not too unhappy with the way they look right now. I did lose about seven pounds these last six weeks.

Moving my hair to the front, I face my fear and walk toward the door, opening it. As soon as I step out, I find a room filled with soft music, dim lights, and an array of lit candles on the large ornate dresser.

"Charlie," I hear his voice coming from the left of the room, how did I not see him? "You are stunning, just stunning."

I immediately look down, my nerves getting the best of me. How does a scar have such control over me? Maybe it's not the scar at all; maybe it's a subconscious fear of this unknown path I am taking. Not even a moment later, I feel Xander's hand on my chin, lifting it up, looking directly into my eyes.

"Don't look down. Let me see you," he says, kissing my lips. "Don't ever hide from me. You are the most beautiful thing I've ever seen."

Next, his eyes make their way to the spot I am hiding with my hair. Kind of stupid of me really, thinking I'm disguising anything, but hey, it's what got me out into this room. His fingers make their way to my neck, touching my hair and slowly moving it. Immediately I take a deep breath, and he counters with a smile. Moving the hair behind my shoulder, his eyes peer down, and I study him, wondering what exactly is going through his mind. He doesn't say a word, but lets his lips do all of the talking by placing them on the top of my scar, slowly kissing a trail as far as the corset allows. Even though I felt stiff as a board, the more his mouth moves on me, the more I feel that I can actually relax. I close my eyes, and my hand finds the back of his neck, my fingers running up the back of his head. Groaning against my skin, his lips travel up, caressing my neck, and I let out a small moan of pleasure. Seconds later, our mouths find each other and fight a war so intense that I can barely catch my breath.

"I want you," he whispers in my ear, and I reply, "I need you."

Lifting me up, he carries me to his bed, setting me down at the edge. Pushing me down so that I am lying on my back, his hands make their way to my thong, gently pulling it down. Right as I feel his hands run up my legs, I close my eyes, letting out a slight moan. Stopping at my upper thighs, he pushes them apart, and immediately, I feel his warm mouth on my entrance, devouring me, quenching his thirst.

His tongue is torturous yet exhilarating at the same time. The moment he starts sucking on my clit, I grip the sheet, and a moan escapes from deep inside of me. The intensity is almost more than I can bear, and my hands move to his shoulders in an attempt to give myself a quick break, but instead, he grips my wrists, slamming them down on the bed next to me, holding them firmly. His tongue continues to play, and I feel myself come undone, quite vocal. Kissing the inside of my thighs, he releases my wrists, slightly running his nails up my arms. That sensation alone makes me want to come again, and before his hands leave mine as he passes my knuckles, I grasp him. He looks at me and smiles, his fingers, slipping through mine, kissing the top of my hand.

"Come here," I whisper, and he gets on the bed, removing his shirt.

I sit up, and my hands immediately make their way to his chest, traveling down toward the black leather belt. Taking my face in his hands, he kisses me, and blindly, I undo the clasp, removing the belt. This kiss is slow but steady, almost mimicking the movement of my hands slowly undoing the button and zipper of his pants. Peeling them down his hips, my hand slips under the waistband of his boxers, gripping his already erect cock and slowly stroking it up and down. He groans into our kiss, and I keep stroking him. Moving his boxers down with my free hand, I give myself more space and run my hand all the way up. For a moment, I stop, what the heck is that?

"What is it?" he asks, and my eyes peer down at his cock, trying to figure out what I felt with my thumb.

"Oh my god, you have a piercing?"

"Ha, yeah. I guess I could have mentioned that before," he grins. "Hope you don't mind."

"Hell no! I love it," I reply, wondering why I sound so excited. It's not like I've ever been with someone that had the head of his cock pierced.

I don't waste any time and begin teasing him with my tongue, right around the piercing.

"Fuck," he groans, moving one of his hands into my hair, gripping it slightly.

Running my tongue down his length on one side, I feel him grip my hair a little harder. Once I arrive back at the tip, I start to run circles all around the head, very slowly. He starts to groan again but seems as if he's holding back just a bit, so I take him into my mouth entirely and begin pleasuring him. His groans continue, and his hand never leaves my hair. His grip loosens a bit, but his dominance is still displayed. Another *fuck* escapes his lips, and right as I move my mouth back up to the head, his grip on me becomes quite firm, and he begins moving his hips forward, pushing his entire cock back into my mouth. For a moment, I feel as if I may gag, maybe because I'm not in control. He slowly moves in and out of my mouth, getting me used to this foreign feeling. Once he's certain that I'm comfortable, he moves harder, and the sensation has me so turned on that I feel myself already dripping with pleasure.

Xander

"Fuck, babe. Don't stop," I groan, and she picks up the momentum.

Releasing the grip on her hair, my head leans back, trying my best to hold back the inevitable. Realizing quickly that if she continues, it will only be mere seconds before I come, I grip her shoulders, throwing her down on the bed next to me, so she lies on her back. Spreading her legs, I wrap my arms around her thighs, pulling her deep into my mouth. My tongue finds her clit, teasing her just as she did me and her moans turn into screams of pleasure. Hell yeah, I love someone who is vocal. Out of the corner of my eye, I see her hand grip the sheet again, and I reach for it, placing it on my cock. Immediately, she starts stroking me, slow and steady, slow and torturous. I start to groan and want nothing more than to be buried deep inside of her. Propping myself up, her hand releases me, and I grip her, turning her around, bringing her up to her knees. Gripping the base of my cock I begin to rub it against her entrance, coating myself with her wetness.

"You want this?" I ask, and she lets out a slight moan.

Before I can react, she reaches through her legs, grabbing me firmly and pushes back, taking me in.

"Who said you were in charge?" I groan, playfully slapping the right side of her ass.

She didn't expect that, but I've been looking forward to this for a long time. I begin to move, thrusting into her, slow but hard, burying myself entirely. Her moans and screams are sending me into ecstasy, and within seconds, my right hand moves to her neck, and I begin moving faster. Using my left

217

hand, I give her another slap, this time, on the left side. This one was a little harder, and I see a partial outline of my hand on her fair skin. This set something off in her because now she takes over, fucking me hard. Normally, I would take back control, but she's letting go, and it's fucking hot. Once I feel myself get close, I grab her neck a little harder, and my other hand grips the rim of the corset at her breast, pulling her up against my chest, biting the back of her neck. Letting out an animalistic groan, I feel myself release into her, and her head falls back on top of my shoulder. I still feel myself pulsate inside of her when suddenly, she clenches down, making me relinquish all I have.

"Fuck babe, why did we wait so long?" I groan.

"I don't know," she replies, panting.

Still in position, still connected, my hand moves onto her chin, turning her head and kissing her deep. Her hand moves to the back of my head, her tongue invading my mouth. I already know that this moment will stay with me as long as I will live.

Chapter 28

Charlie

I can't even begin to describe what I am feeling right now. Lying in Xander's arms, him holding me close, hearing his heartbeat, there's no place I'd rather be. I've been looking forward to this day for some time, and it topped anything I ever imagined. For one, I have never fucked doggy style nor had oral sex during a first encounter; it always ended up being missionary. With Xander, it just flowed naturally. He made me forget everything from my scar to even my surroundings. I felt...safe. I remember asking him what it meant to be a submissive, and one of the things he brought up was him keeping me safe. At the time, I had no idea what the hell he was talking about. Now I am starting to understand, and if I reach into myself, I can honestly say that I'm craving more. I want to experience the things we talk about, with him, and only him.

As my head rests on his chest, I trace an imaginary zig-zag line down Xander's ribcage, making him chuckle just a bit. Kissing the top of my head, he runs his hand up and down my back. We've been lying here in silence, recovering from maybe one of the best nights of my life. Suddenly, Xander speaks.

"Are you all right?"

"I'm great, you?" I ask.

"I'm fine. I want to make sure you are ok. How's your ass?"

"My ass?" I ask, a little confused.

"Yes, your ass, where I spanked you."

"Oh, yeah. I'm good," I reply, totally forgetting that happened for a moment, but now that I think of it, what a turn on.

"Can I get you anything? Something to drink?"

"Why are you asking all of these questions?" I ask, propping myself up on his chest, looking into his eyes.

"It's called aftercare. It's where I need to make sure you are taken care of and feel 100%. If not, then it's my job to get you there."

"Just for slapping my ass?" I say, raising an eyebrow.

"Of course," he says in a serious tone, looking at me like I have three heads. "It's pertinent that you receive aftercare after a scene, and just know, I would never just get up and leave your side."

"Was that a scene?"

"Well, not really," he replies.

"When will this scene happen?"

"You think you're ready?"

"Maybe," I counter, and he smiles.

"Let's learn to walk before we start to run."

"You're probably right," I sigh. "Oh, can I ask you something? It's kind of stupid."

"Shoot."

"Did your piercing hurt?" I ask.

"My piercing? No, not really. I have a high pain tolerance, though."

"It just seemed so sensitive to the touch," I begin. "Or better yet, tongue, I figured it had to hurt like hell."

"Oh, I will admit, your tongue was driving me wild and yes, super sensitive for sure. An amazing feeling! What did you think?"

"I loved playing with it," I admit, giggling.

I return my head to his chest, and he inhales deeply. Lying there quietly, not a word is said for the next five minutes, though it feels as if we are communicating on a different level. No awkward silence at all, it's a beautiful one.

"Xander?" I begin.

"Yes, babe."

"I felt so ... what' the word?"

"Connected?" he replies.

"Exactly, connected. Almost like I can feel your thoughts and completely read my mind."

"That's the bond I was telling you about. I feel it too," he explains, kissing my head.

"Gosh, and to think I assumed this was all about hurting people," I comment. "There's so much more, so much people don't know."

"Agreed, most people don't even care to find out. I do believe that our relationships are much deeper in the lifestyle than compared to a vanilla couple."

"Just through talking," I say.

"Yes, that's the basis, and it never stops. Never."

"That's amazing. I love that," I say, kissing his chest.

"Even though communication is the basis, and we work toward a bond, it's not all fun and games."

"What do you mean?" I ask.

"It gets difficult at times. We are learning about each other. I am discovering and studying you, your reactions, your body language, and more. This brings me to a point. Even though we aren't doing any scenes yet, you need to think of a safe word."

"I remember you talking about that before," I begin. "So, if something goes wrong, in my opinion, or I'm uncomfortable, I use the safe word?

"Yes," he replies.

"You can stop immediately? Like, let's say we are in the middle of having sex."

"I stop as soon as you say the word."

"Wow, isn't it difficult?"

"Of course, it is, but your wellbeing is my priority, always will be," Xander explains, and I'm amazed at that amount of self-control.

Lying on his chest, I have many things running through my mind. What just happened was probably the hottest thing I've ever experienced sexually. Sure, for him, that was probably very *vanilla* as he likes to say, but for me, it was new. I take a deep breath and run my fingers down his ribcage, and a small groan escapes his lips. He is sound asleep, but his grip on me is still tight. For a moment, I wonder just how intense everything could get. What if we find out I can't handle it? Would we have to part ways? No, we had this discussion, we would make things work...somehow.

Chapter 29

Charlie

This weekend went by too quickly, and I had such a difficult time saying goodbye to Xander. Part of me wishes I would have taken tomorrow off, so I would have had just one more night with him. One more night cradled in his arms, feeling his breath against my neck, the way his thumb circles on my lower back when we lie in bed talking to one another. At least there wasn't any traffic on the way back home, and I actually made it back in record time. As I begin to unpack my bag, I find a folded piece of paper inside, and a smile comes to my lips. When did he do this? Unfolding the piece of paper, it reads, *What I have with you I don't want with anyone else.* I can feel my eyes water just a bit, and I look up to the ceiling to fight the tears. Taking a deep breath, my eyes peer back down at the note, tracing his letters with my finger. No one has ever said anything like this to me, at least not this directly. Sometimes I find him a little hard to read, and something as simple as a note reassures me what he feels. I will admit, an *I love you* almost slipped before leaving, but I stopped myself. Obviously, he doesn't throw that term around, but I wonder if he feels as if he could go into that direction with me. I know I could ask; he always tells me to be open and honest. Chuckling, I remember him telling me he would never consider any question stupid or laughable, so I should just ask away. No, I can't. What if I don't like the answer? What if I would be left a heartbroken mess?

Grabbing my phone off my bed, I send Xander a message, telling him the note was one of the best surprises I've ever received. Within seconds my phone chimes, and he replies that he misses me terribly. Oh Xander, why do we have to live so far apart?

After finishing my laundry, I call Leah, asking if she wants to grab dinner in a bit, and just as I figured, she agrees. We decide to try a new restaurant that just opened about a week ago near Leah's apartment. I arrive a few minutes early, and since it seems a bit on the busy side, I go inside and give the hostess my name. As soon as Leah shows up, she tells me she has some exciting news, and I'm assuming that she must have met someone new. About five minutes later, the hostess leads us to a table for two and hands us menus. Once the waiter takes our drink order, I look at Leah, telling her to spit it out.

"Oh yeah," she begins. "I got a job offer."

"That's awesome. I know you've been looking for something new for a while. Where will you be working?"

"It's in San Diego actually," Leah explains, and my eyes widen.

"What?"

"Yeah, I'll be in your old stomping grounds," she smiles. "Or close to them."

"Wow," I say, a little shocked. "First off, congratulations, I'm happy for you."

"Thank you. The pay is amazing, and you can't beat the location. Sun, beach, good times."

"Definitely. My god, I am going to miss you so much," I say, walking over to her side, giving her a hug.

"I know, that is the only drawback. I've lived in Baltimore my entire life, so it's a huge change. I'm going to miss you too, girl."

"So, when is the big move?" I say, wiping a little tear from my eye.

"It's not for another month, I still have to sign some paperwork and organize a few things," Leah replies, getting a bit emotional. "Anyway, how was your weekend with Xander?"

"It was amazing, he's amazing. We took a walk on the beach, went out to dinner, he read me a few passages of the book he is working on."

"Another PG-rated weekend, you guys should wear purity rings," Leah teases.

"Very funny," I chuckle. "You know I like to keep those things private."

"Oh, so something did happen," she says, wiggling her eyebrows.

"Not telling," I reply, rolling my eyes.

"No worries, you just did," she laughs, and I huff, knowing I just gave it all away.

After getting home, I call Xander and tell him about Leah's upcoming plans, and he asks me how I feel about it. Leah and I have been close since I moved to Baltimore, and I can't imagine her not being here. I know I still have Brynn and Rachel, but my relationship with them isn't quite as close. Right now, I wish Xander lived a bit closer; I hate having a long-distance relationship with him. Even though we talk non-stop during the day, it's the nights that are very lonely. I love laying in his arms as he holds me, the way he kisses the top of my head, the way he makes me feel safe and secure.

Xander: I know it's hard to lose someone that is close to you, but at least she won't be too far from where your family lives, right?

Charlie: Yes, you're right, actually. We could meet up when I fly home for a visit.

Xander: Yes, and knowing the two of you, you'll be in constant contact.

Charlie: Probably, though I will say that you take up a lot of my time.

Xander: Is that a bad thing?

Charlie: Oh no. If you lived closer, I would try to see you every day!

Xander: That's what I like to hear.

Charlie: You would probably get sick of me.

Xander: Never. I can't get enough of you, Charlie.

Charlie: Well, that's what I like to hear.

Xander: So, any plans for the rest of the night?

Charlie: No, just talk to you, and then go to bed.

Xander: Same here. Oh, so I have something else I want to tell you about.

Charlie: I'm all ears.

Xander: Ok, Subdrop, and Subspace.

Charlie: I remember seeing that during one of my searches but didn't really research it.

Xander: Well, Subdrop can happen after an intense scene when hormones and chemicals are running haywire. It's possible to slip into an almost like depressive state. It can happen immediately or even days later. That is why aftercare is so important.

Charlie: Is it really that bad?

Xander: It can be, sure. That is why it is so important that I make sure you are safe. Even though we didn't technically have a scene, how would you have felt if I had just gotten up and walked off and left you there alone, without a touch or words spoken?

Charlie: Uncomfortable and maybe insecure.

Xander: Yup. Now imagine some of the intense plays I've told you about.

Charlie: Oh wow, yeah.

Xander: See, that's why aftercare is so crucial. I will continue to check on you until I know you are 100%. I never want you to experience Subdrop and will do everything in my power to prevent it. Though, it could still happen, even with the best preparation.

Charlie: You seriously are amazing. I trust you will. What is the other?

Xander: Subspace is when you are completely immersed in the moment, and you forget everything else around you. You can let go and just enjoy. Some people say it's almost as if they are in a trance. You may even want to try things you've never imagined before because your mind will be in an altered state. It will be up to me to monitor your mental and physical safety. Very important.

Charlie: Wow, it sounds very intense.

Xander: It is.

Charlie: So, I have a question.

Xander: Yes?

Charlie: I remember you mentioning these limits. If I happened to enter this state of not being reasonable, would you still respect my limits?

Xander: I'm glad you bring this up. Of course, I would respect your limits, always. Hard limits are there for a reason. Sure, after a while, we can always discuss them to see where you stand with them, but nothing happens unless it's discussed and agreed upon.

Charlie: Hard limit, right. Wasn't there another one?

Xander: Yes, soft limits. Soft limits are things you may not see yourself doing right now but could possibly in the future.

Charlie: I see.

Xander: I have a challenge for you.

Charlie: Yes.

Xander: Wow, no protest?

Charlie: Have to change it up once in a while.

Xander: Ha-ha, ok! I want you to make your personal list, soft and hard limits. Obviously, you haven't experienced most of it yet, but I'd like to see where you stand.

Charlie: How much time do I have?

Xander: Two days.

Charlie: Thank you.

Xander: Of course.

Xander

I'm baffled that I haven't given this challenge before now. Normally I do this close to the beginning since it's a way to test compatibility. Then again, how can I be surprised? Charlie knew very little when we started, practically nothing. Now is the perfect time. She's learned so much over these months and now has more of a picture. Sure, she still hasn't personally experienced these things, but she can make an assumption about it.

I am really interested to see this list. A part of me thinks that it will be five pages long, five pages of hard limits, that is. I have my fingers crossed that the collar doesn't appear on either list. I would love to use it during our first session. If it is, I will have to respect it and hope that she may change her mind with time and guidance. Deep down inside, I know that caning will be on her hard limit list. After the story I told her about Melany, I'm sure I've scarred her for life. Let's hope not; I love using the cane as well.

Chapter 30

Charlie

Well, I have to say I am very pleased with myself. I didn't find this challenge too difficult, and I'm sure nothing on my list will come as a surprise to Xander. We've talked about most of the things I would be willing to try and what is a total no for me. He sent me a few links to different websites for more information, just in case I needed it.

While the children are out in the lunchroom, I decide to go over my list one last time on my phone.

<u>Soft limits</u>

Anal

Ankle restraints

Pet Play

Hair pulling

Daddy Dom/Little Girl

<u>Hard limits</u>

Caning

Belt

Fisting

Breath Play/Choking

Threesomes

Knife Play

Public Exposure

Video Taping

Rape Scenes

Anything involving blood, urine, and feces

Slave Scenes

Yep. Looks good to me. I can't really think of anything that I would add for now. Looking at the clock, I notice that the kids should be returning in about two minutes, so I send my list to Xander before placing my phone back into the desk. I'm sure I'll have a bunch of disappointed faces staring back at me in less than ten minutes because I am about to give a surprise math test. I will admit, when I was in school, I loved those times. Math always was my favorite subject, so it was more like a treat than a downer.

Leah actually got a phone call from her soon to be boss this morning, asking if there is any way she can start next week instead of next month. Now it's definitely real, she is going to be gone, so soon too. After work, I make my way to Leah's apartment to help pack her things. She has a lot of small knick-knacks, mostly breakable, so that means lots of wrapping. Rachel will be there as well, and Brynn said she would try to make it tomorrow. As I come to her door, I see it's wide open, and she has empty boxes everywhere.

"Hey Charlie, thank you so much for helping out. This is so last minute," Leah says, giving me a hug.

"God damn Leah, why do you have so much shit?" Rachel announces, walking into the living room from Leah's bedroom. "Oh, hey Charlie."

"Hey," I reply as she walks into the kitchen and opens a bottle of wine.

"We will definitely need this," Rachel jokes. "When is your flight?"

"It's next Wednesday," Leah replies.

"You really want to pack everything? Won't you have some things you still need?" I ask.

"Yeah, like TV, pots and pans?" Rachel adds.

"Nope, I will be staying with my parents until I leave so everything can get packed. All of the things I need like clothes and documents are already at their house."

"Sounds good, let's get started," I say, grabbing a box and making my way into the kitchen.

My phone chimes, and I see it's a message from Xander, asking me to let him know when I get home so we can talk about my list. Now I wonder if I passed this challenge, his message was quite straight-forward. Well, of course, I did, it's my list, my limits. After replying, I put my phone back on the counter and grab all of Leah's glasses out of the cabinet and start wrapping them in packing paper.

"Knock-knock," Brynn says as she comes into the door.

"Oh wow, I thought you said you couldn't make it," Leah says, her hands on her hips.

"Well, technically, I can't. Ryan's daughter has this thing tonight, but I thought I would be a good friend and drop off dinner for you guys."

"You read my mind," Rachel sighs, and Brynn comes in, setting a bag on the counter.

"It's nothing special. Just some grocery store sushi," Brynn smiles.

"Perfect," I reply, and the four of us grab a tray and sit on the couch...and floor.

While eating, Brynn tells us about something Ryan wanted to try in the bedroom last night, and a small grin comes over my face. She said he wanted to try handcuffs, and she was completely against it.

"Well, how would you guys have reacted?" she asks.

"Not really my thing," Rachel agrees.

"You all know I'm a freak," Leah laughs, almost choking on her sushi roll.

"How about you, Charlie?" Brynn asks.

"Well. I wouldn't have turned it down. It could be interesting," I say, and Rachel makes a face.

"Are you telling me if Xander said he wanted to tie you up and fuck you, you would be willing to try?" Brynn asks. "Giving up control?"

"Well, you have to trust the person you're with. Yes, I wouldn't have an issue with it. I think it's important to be openminded."

"Wow, I'm surprised," Rachel exclaims.

"Why?"

"You guys have only seen each other a few times, how can you say you trust him?" Rachel asks.

"We talk all the time; nothing is off limits. I feel like I know him better than all of my past boyfriends combined."

"I suppose this guy has it really easy," Brynn huffs.

"Why do you say that?" I ask, a little irritated.

"Well, he can paint you a really nice picture while he lives hours away, and the weekends you spend together are probably always great. Try living with the guy, completely different story," Brynn explains.

"Ok, you're acting like I've never lived with a guy before," I reply.

"How do you think the two of you will carry on your relationship with the distance between you?" Rachel asks.

"It's not that far. Sure, if things continue, one of us will probably have to think about moving," I respond. "I have no issue moving to the beach."

"Hell yeah, girl," Leah says, giving me a high five. "Don't let these bitches get you down. You have a gem there."

After we finish our sushi, Brynn leaves, and the three of us get back to the tedious task of packing. I manage to finish the entire kitchen with Rachel's help, and Leah took care of all of the pictures and breakables. It's already 9 pm when I finally get to my apartment, and I'm exhausted, but I know I still have to call Xander. I decide to run a bath so I can just soak and talk to him at the same time. As the water fills the tub, Brynn's statement runs through my head; *he can paint you a pretty picture while he lives hours away.* She's right, he could, but he doesn't. I can't expect her to understand the close bond we share. I can't fault her, or the others. I don't mention Xander very much. Of course, we talk about him here and there, but I can't share most of our conversations with them, nor would I want to.

Once the tub is full, I turn off the water, undress, and slip into the tub. Mmm... this is heaven. Reaching for my phone and headphones on the toilet, I put one into my ear and hit the call button before putting the phone back on the toilet lid.

Xander: Hey babe, long day for you.

Charlie: Yes, it was. I'm soaking in the tub right now.

Xander: What I would give to be there.

Charlie: I even have bubbles.

Xander: Mmm...damn. I'm missing out.

Charlie: Yes, you are. So, how was my list?

Xander: It was good for starters.

Charlie: For starters?

Xander: Yup. Though, one thing on your hard limit list just about broke my heart.

Charlie: Which one?

Xander: Caning.

Charlie: I knew it.

Xander: Fuck, I love doing that, but I respect it. Who knows, you may change your mind later.

Charlie: Fat chance.

Xander: We will see. So, fire plays, Saint Andrews Cross, the horse...not on your lists. Those are ok with you?

Charlie: Fire plays, hell no. The cross is that thing where you're tied up, right? Is the horse something similar to gym class?

Xander: Hold on. I'll send you some pictures and GIFs.

Charlie: Ok.

Xander: You should have them.

Charlie: I remember that one from the club.

Xander: That's the cross and hold on, now you should have the horse.

Charlie: Cross, maybe. Horse, I do not like.

Xander: Don't worry, this comes way later anyway if you choose to explore it. How about wax plays?

Charlie: Dripping hot wax on my body?

Xander: Yes.

Charlie: I think I would love that.

Xander: I would love to do it to you.

Charlie: *chuckles*

Xander: Charlie?

Charlie: Yes?

Xander: Why do I get the feeling that you are blushing right now?

Charlie: Maybe because I am. Damn, you know me well.

Xander: We know each other.

Charlie: You're right. Hey, by the way, what are your hard limits?

Xander: I am open to a lot, but my list definitely includes Golden Showers, Scat play and actually threesomes. I'm not into multiple partners anymore. Also, I would never have more than one sub at a time.

Charlie: Wait, Golden Shower has something to do with pee. What is scat play?

Xander: Feces.

Charlie: Oh, that's right. So gross.

Xander: To each their own.

Charlie: Well, I'm so relieved you're not into threesomes anymore. I was a little afraid that I wouldn't be enough in the long run.

Xander: You are all I want, all I need. Besides, threesomes bring issues, temptation, and aren't as great as they make them look in porn. Oh, I was surprised to see DDLG on your soft limit list. I recall a conversation where you said you can't picture calling me Daddy.

Charlie: I still can't. During our talks about the various lifestyles, this one just seems like it could be fun. By the way, do you like to be called anything? Like Sir or Master?

Xander: Not really. Though for some reason, the thought of you calling me Sir is definitely turning me on. Something we can think about.

Charlie: Oh good.

Xander: What?

Charlie: I prefer Sir over Master.

Xander

Chuckling to myself, I toss the phone beside me on the bed. I knew this conversation was going to take a turn as soon as I found out she was in the tub. Suppose I will have to throw the comforter in the washer tonight. I've made quite a mess here, or better yet, she did. Getting up, I go into the bathroom to wash my hands before pulling off the comforter. Bunching it up, I throw it into the washer along with some soap and hit start.

I was very pleased with her list and what do you know, the collar and leash weren't on there. I think that's what made my day for sure. I may have been a little premature, but I 've already bought Charlie's collar. Black leather with a silver buckle and a small padlock on the back. Next to each side of the buckle is a letter made of up gems, X and C, Xander, and Charlie.

Part of me wasn't all that surprised to find DDLG on her soft limit list. She has some tendencies of a little, and who knows, maybe we will explore it one day. One shocker was Pet Play, even though I didn't bring it up. I've done it, but it never was my thing. Hell, if she wants to dress up like a kitten and sit in a cage, I can be more than accommodating. Maybe I'll enjoy it with her, who knows.

Chapter 31

Charlie

I need him...badly. In these last two months, we've been able to see each other much more, which is amazing, though, the more I see him, the more I long for him. I chuckle when I think about my last visit to Ocean City. I barely even made it through the door, and our clothes came flying off. He had me pinned against the wall, devouring me right then and there. Even though we keep things vanilla, the passion between us is unbelievable. Yesterday we had a conversation about something called consideration time. He told me it's the next step after vetting, and the name itself raises questions inside me. Of course, he made the entire thing into a task. *What does consideration time mean to me?*

Sitting at my table with a pen and paper, I try my best to get a few sentences together, but it's useless. I think I may be taking it too literally. He explained it to me, but is he really just considering me during this time? Being told I'm under consideration doesn't sit well with me for some reason. I suppose I will be failing this task.

About twenty minutes later, my doorbell rings and my heart jumps, partially for joy and the other due to being nervous because I didn't complete my task. Walking to my door, I unlock and open it to find those gorgeous eyes staring back at me with a smile that makes me forget my name.

"Come here, babe," Xander says, pulling me in for a kiss.

"We're taking this inside though, right?" I ask, jokingly, well maybe not, I'm sure he would have no problem fucking me right in the entryway.

"Hmm, good question. Care to try something new?" he asks, winking at me, and I roll my eyes, pulling him inside.

"How was your drive?" I ask as he sets his bags on the floor next to the couch.

"Small talk first, all right," he laughs, and I give him a funny expression. "It wasn't bad. I had to take the alternate route since my app showed a few accidents with about an hour delay. Thank god for technology."

"Definitely," I say, leaning against the table, arms folded.

"What's wrong?" he asks, eyes focused on my body language.

"Wrong? Nothing, why?"

"You seem different, did something happen?" he counters, walking up to me and placing his hands on my arms.

"Ok," I sigh. "I didn't complete the task."

"Why?" he asks, looking into my eyes.

"I tried, but the more I sat there pondering about it, the more I couldn't get my thoughts to line up."

"I can see it's troubling you, come, let's sit down," he offers, holding my hand and leading me to the couch. "Tell me what is on your mind."

"Ok. Consideration time. It just seems so...business-like."

"Business-like?" he asks.

"Yes, kind of like a transaction," I begin. "I just feel like we are more than just...damn, I can't think of the word."

"You feel that this is a romantic relationship," he replies, and now I'm on pins and needles.

"Yes," I reply, hoping I don't ruin it all.

"Charlie," he takes a deep breath. "We've grown very close. Like I said in the beginning, I am a Dom, and I am looking for a sub. I live this lifestyle; it's who I am."

"Fuck," I reply.

"No fuck, let me finish," he says, grabbing my hand. "I didn't expect a romantic relationship to develop to be quite honest, but it has. My feelings for you are very, very strong."

"Phew, thank god, but can I ask, why consideration time? If we both consider this a relationship, is there really a need for this next step?"

"What we have right now is a *normal* relationship, something you know I like to call vanilla. We are working our way to the BDSM lifestyle, so things change and continue to evolve."

"What if during that time I don't meet all the guidelines, I don't want to lose you."

"No, you won't lose me," he replies in a sharp tone.

"So, it will just be ok if I say it's not for me?"

"We will work on it, take steps back when needed. This isn't a race, and there is no finish line. There is always room to learn, to step back, to re-examine. I still find myself learning things every day."

"What exactly happens during this time?"

"Consideration time is about growing even closer to each other and strengthening our bond. You will see that it becomes more intense, more serious. I know in the past we have been quite playful, and don't get me wrong; I love that, but I will be more direct, and my expectations will be higher. Punishments will be different as well. Basically, everything we have talked about will be put into action, not all at once, of course."

"With you being more direct, are you talking about when we have sex?"

"Of course, but don't worry, I won't be using that cane on you right from the start, well, maybe."

"Maybe? Hey, it's a hard limit, buddy."

"There are ways to use it during sensual play, which I believe you will love. It's not all about pain, remember?" he explains, running a finger down my arm.

"Yes, I remember," I reply, taking a deep breath. "So, sensual plays, are you talking candles and romantic music?"

"Oh babe, so much more. Sure, we can have that, but sensual plays involve anything from feather plays to ice cubes."

"Wow, that sounds really exciting," I reply, biting my lip.

"It is, and that is where we will begin once you're ready."

"Really? We begin with sensual play?" I ask.

"Unless you want to be strapped to the St. Andrews Cross and teased with the wand, also an option."

"Nope," I say quickly. "I'm good with the step by step."

"Have you thought of a safe word yet?" Xander asks.

"I'm sorry," I admit. "I'm so bad at this. Do you have any recommendations?"

"It's up to you, it's your word, and you have to be comfortable with it."

"How about stop?" I ask, and he makes a face. "What's wrong with stop?"

"Everything. Remember when I was sucking your clit the last time, and you kept saying stop?"

"Yeah," I reply, and it becomes clear.

"You didn't want me to stop."

"You're right, so another word. I swear I will have one the next time you ask."

Chapter 32

Charlie

As we lay in bed, I listen to his heartbeat, trying to etch it into my mind so I can remember it during the time we are separated. I'm exhausted though my mind will not rest, consumed with thoughts about what's to come in our future. I am a little afraid of the unknown, but I also know that Xander will guide me every step of the way. A smile comes to my face thinking about our conversation at dinner. I asked, and he delivered. To tell the truth, I like him being direct and stern. There's something about his eyes that change, giving him total authority, making me want to please him. When he ordered me to kneel and undo his pants last night, I felt myself tingle, every inch of me. Maybe I am ready for this? I won't know unless I try. Maybe I'll bring this up over breakfast.

The alarm on my phone rings, and it's 6:30 am, and for a moment, I swipe it to the off position and rest my head back on the pillow. A second later, I remember why it's set in the first place. Xander gave me the task of getting up and make breakfast. Jumping up, I find my panties on the ground, putting them on. Finding my shirt is a challenge; I can't remember where that flew last night. Walking over to my dresser, I just grab a new one, and that's when I hear shuffling in the bed. I turn around, and Xander is sitting up.

"Good morning Xander," I say, and he smiles.

"Good morning, babe. What are you doing?"

"Well, I am about to go make breakfast, and I can't find my shirt, so I'm grabbing a new one."

"No, you're not."

"I'm not?" I question.

"You are going into the kitchen and making breakfast just wearing your panties."

"You're being serious?"

"Absolutely," I want to enjoy that view for as long as I can.

"Ok then," I say, putting the shirt back into the dresser and walking out of the bedroom.

Getting the eggs, bacon, and butter out of the refrigerator, I grab a bowl out of the cabinet and start cracking the eggs. Right when I begin whisking them, Xander appears, wearing his boxer shorts. For a moment, I look at him and then return my eyes to the bowl. Suddenly, I can feel him behind me, his hands on my waist before one of them runs down to my thigh. I sigh but continue whisking the eggs like it's not phasing me. Next, he moves my hair to the left and his mouth, exploring my neck, running his tongue up to my ear, and I stop for a moment.

"Continue," he demands, and I put some butter in the pan.

I regain my composure and reach for the salt and pepper in the cabinet above me, placing them on the counter. Before I know it, his finger invades me, and his thumb moves on my clit. How in the hell am I supposed to make us breakfast? He is setting me up for failure. With my hands braced on the counter, I close my eyes, and a moan escapes my lips, fuck, what is he doing to me? Pressed close against my back, I feel his hard cock against me, turning me on to the point where I just want him to throw me on the table or whatever else is close.

"Charlie," he says. "Who told you to stop cooking?"

God damn, the butter is melted. I pour the egg mixture into the pan, hearing the sizzle. That is the moment he starts to work me harder, biting my neck. I know it won't take long for me to come, but I need to make sure I don't burn these eggs. My moans become more audible, and I drop the utensil I was holding to move the eggs around.

"Don't come," he demands, and it takes everything in me not to tell him to stop. I just have to learn to control myself, even if his fingers are fucking me like there's no tomorrow.

Grabbing a new utensil out of the drawer, I cook the eggs and place four pieces of bread into the toaster, pressing down the handle. His thumb is really working my clit, and I instinctively start to close my legs to try to change the position he has on me, but all I get in return is a slap on my thigh and a firm no. Taking a deep breath, I turn off the burner to the eggs, since they are very well done, and move the pan off the burner. The toast pops up, and I turn to him.

"Breakfast is ready," I announce, and he smirks, removing his hand from in between my legs and licking his fingers.

"It smells delicious, but after tasting this, I think I changed my mind," he smiles, turning me around so that my back is against the counter.

Pulling my panties down, he kneels down in front of me and spreads my thighs with his hands. His tongue begins to torture my already swollen sex lips, alternating between licking and gently sucking. One of my hands grips the counter while the other is in his hair, gripping it, making him groan. My head leans back, and I enjoy the pleasure he is giving me. I feel myself begin to throb, and the hand that was entangled in his hair now moves to the other side of me, gripping the counter hard. Suddenly I feel his mouth move to my clit, using his fingers to enter me once again. How can I not come like this? I begin to pant, trying to control myself, but the urge to come is getting stronger and stronger.

"Xander," I barely make out.

"You can come," I hear him say, his mouth still between my legs.

A moment later, I let go, screaming in both pleasure and agony. This orgasm is so intense, and I feel myself explode all over him. My legs begin to shake just a bit, and I feel his hand rub my thigh up and down. Once my breathing returns to normal, he removes his mouth from me and stands up, giving me a big smile.

"How about those eggs now?" he asks, and I completely forgot I cooked eggs. Fuck, he drives me insane.

"Well, I'm sure they are cold now," I say, grabbing the pan with my panties still around my ankles.

"That's what microwaves are for," he says, grabbing the pan from me and emptying the eggs onto a plate to put them into the microwave.

Sitting down at the table, by the way, I've pulled my panties up again, and I watch Xander as he bites into the toast.

"You did very well," he comments, making me smile. "Though you forgot something."

"What? What do you mean?" I ask, looking around the table. "Did you say you wanted ketchup? I told you I don't have any."

"Nope, try to think. What did you forget?"

"I have no idea. We have eggs, toast, juice... oh shit!" I say as I realize what didn't make it on the table, nor the pan. "The bacon."

"Yes," he laughs. "Don't worry; I put it back in the fridge."

"I'm sorry," I say, upset at myself for overlooking it.

"No worries, really. It's probably better you didn't cook it while naked anyway. Grease burns are nasty, and I prefer wax plays."

"I'd love to try that," I admit, wiping my mouth with a napkin.

"We will," he counters with a big smile.

"Xander, can I ask you something?"

"Of course, babe, what is it?"

"I thought about our conversation yesterday, you know, about consideration time. I think I'm ready to go there," I say, wondering how he will react.

"You think you're ready?"

"Well, yes. I think the only way I will know is if I get to experience it. You've prepared me as well as you can, and though talking is the basis, it's hard to form any kind of opinion without experiencing it."

"Let me ask you something," he says, sitting back in his chair, looking at me. "How did you feel about me being stern?"

"Honestly?" I ask.

"Always babe."

"I loved it," I admit. "It was a turn on for sure."

"Really? Well, I'm glad to hear that."

"So, do you think I'm ready?"

"Did you choose a safe word?"

"Thorn."

"Thorn? That's actually a good one, I like it," Xander says. "Here's the deal. Since I have to leave here in a few hours to head back home, I believe we should take this next week to think about it, and I mean, really think. On Friday night, you'll be coming to see me anyway so we can figure things out then. What do you think?"

"Sounds great!"

Chapter 33

Charlie

I've taken the week to think everything over, re-read some of our chats, emails. Looked through the written tasks he has given me over these months, and now more than ever do I want to experience the next stage. During the week, Xander and I revisited some of our prior conversations and asked how I feel about the collar and leash. I remember thinking it was degrading before, but after one of our talks about the meaning, it's become something I feel myself yearning for. To be honest, it is just beautiful, and I would be so proud to wear one for him.

Damn, this drive is taking forever today. It seems as if everyone is going int the direction of Ocean City. Well, I'll get there eventually. As I'm stuck in another traffic jam my phone rings and I answer it with the button on my steering wheel.

Charlie: Hello?

Leah: Hey girl, just wanted to see how you are.

Charlie: Leah! I'm great. On the way to Xander's right now.

Leah: Awesome. I'm just getting off work right now. I still can't believe you left Cali for Baltimore. I'm declaring you insane.

Charlie: So, I see you're still loving it.

Leah: Hell yeah! I practically live at the beach now. How are Rachel and Brynn? I never seem to catch them at a good time.

Charlie: Well, Brynn is super consumed with Ryan; I think marriage is in the future there. Rachel and I have been out once or twice, but she's been busy with her job and dates. It sucks not having you here.

Leah: I'm so sorry, gosh, I miss you too. I haven't really met anyone here yet to hang with. Some of my coworkers are nice but it will just take time. I'll try to get back to Baltimore on Thanksgiving.

Charlie: Oh, that's great! That's just about a month away. I can't wait.

Leah: So, you'll be in Baltimore? I thought you may spend it with Xander.

Charlie: You know, we haven't discussed that yet. Good point, I'll bring it up.

Leah: Ok, well my food is ready, so I have to run, talk soon!

Charlie: Yes, take care, Leah.

It was so great to hear from her. We do make it a point to call at least twice a week, even if it's just short. We practically text most of the time anyway, but Leah's job is a bit more demanding over there, and the four-hour time difference doesn't always make it very convenient.

An hour later, I finally make it to Xander's house. He really must think I am a slow driver since I always get here late. Grabbing my bag out of the trunk, I shut it, and I already see him coming toward me to grab it from me.

"Babe, you're here," he says, hugging me tightly.

"Fucking traffic again, maybe I need to leave a little later," I say, and he shakes his head.

"Hell no, I already worry about you being on the road right now. You driving here at night, I do not like at all," he replies, grabbing my bag and heading toward the house.

Walking in, I set my keys and purse on the entryway table as he brings my stuff into his bedroom. When he returns, he asks if I've eaten, and I shake my head. Walking to the refrigerator, he pulls out a big container with chicken salad and sets it on the table. I grab two plates out of the cabinet, placing them on the table as well.

"Do you want crackers?" he asks as he takes forks out of the drawer.

"Sure," I reply. "So, what did you do today?"

"Oh, regular work stuff, a little writing, and I also went for a jog on the beach. How about you?"

"Just work. The kids and I did this cool art project with paper-mâché I found online. We are attempting to make piggy banks. Have to see how they turn out next week," I say, laughing since mine looked a bit distorted.

"You are so creative, no wonder the kids love you," Xander smiles.

"I like to keep it interesting. I hate doing the same boring things. We do have some leeway, especially when it comes to art, so why not?"

"I agree, creativity is very important; in any way, shape, and or form."

"So, I talked to Leah on the way here," I begin.

"Oh yeah? How is she?"

"She's great, still loving it there. She said she wants to try to make it to Baltimore for Thanksgiving next month. Do you have any plans for then?"

"Usually, I fly to Florida to spend it with my mom and some other family, but this year she's taking a cruise, so I hadn't really thought about it."

"Would you like to spend it with me?" I ask, hoping he will say yes.

"Of course, I would, definitely. Please just don't drag me shopping the next morning," he says jokingly.

"No worries, I don't do that anyway."

"Phew, lucky me," he replies, playfully wiping imaginary sweat from his forehead. "Have you had time to think things over?"

"In terms of consideration time?"

"Yes. I'm curious to know how you're feeling about it now."

"The same, I still want to take that next step with you, as long as you'll be patient with me since I'm not a sub."

"Of course, I will be patient. I can't expect you to know how everything works. I have given you a good baseline, and it's a start. You just have to make sure that you are willing to give it all you have. No excuses or saying no right off the bat."

"I understand. Do I just say hard limit?" I reply, and he begins to take a deep breath. "I'm kidding; it was a joke. Yes, I know what you mean, no whining. I will try my best."

"That is all I ask," he smiles. "Also, here is another thing I haven't mentioned. Meta Talks."

"What is that?"

"It's a time we won't be in our Dom/sub roles, and we can speak about things, kind of like a time out."

"So, like vanilla?"

"In a sense, yes," Xander replies. "Though, if at any time you feel the need to use your safe word, you can say you need a meta talk, and we can discuss what is going on."

"So why have this term if we talk about things anyway?"

"It's designed, so the Dom doesn't feel like the sub is trying to top from the bottom."

"What does that mean? Top from the bottom?"

"Topping from the bottom means that you as the sub, the bottom, tries to take control in situations where you don't have to," Xander explains.

"Oh ok, yes. I remember you saying something like that before," I reply. "Ok, Meta Talks, got it."

"You look so cute when you're concentrating," Xander says, getting up and grabbing my hand.

"Are we doing this now?" I ask, my heart beating like mad.

"Yes. I am about to tie you to my bed, wrists and ankles, blindfold you and flog the shit out of you," he replies, and my eyes widen. "Silly girl, I'm kidding. No, we are going to go lay down and rest. You worked all day and drove for the last four hours, and I know you're tired."

"You're right, I am," I reply, yawning just a bit.

"Tomorrow is a new day, and it will be a good one since I get to wake up next to you."

"I wish I would never have to leave you again. I have a hard time falling asleep without you," I admit.

"Same here, my love, same here," Xander sighs.

Xander

This is it; she's ready. This has been the shortest vetting time I've ever experienced, but I feel as if I know her better than any of my other subs. I've had time to think about how I will introduce her, and I think I will stick with my original plan. We are not in a race, slow steps. Some might think I'm taking it too easy on her, but I don't fucking care. We do what feels right to us; no one else matters. I want her to love it, not run away in fear.

After dinner, we spend the evening at the beach, taking a walk, sitting in the sand, talking. I can tell she is nervous but determined at the same time. As we sit there, she searches for my touch, and I notice it calms her. After all this time, I can read her like a book, page by page. She is by far my favorite novel, my muse, my everything. A moment later, a thought hits me, and I chuckle.

"What is it?" Charlie asks, turning her head and looking into my eyes.

"I was just thinking," I reply. "When we first started messaging, did you imagine finding yourself here?"

"Hell no," she laughs. "To tell the truth, when I sent you that friend request, I thought you might accept, and then I'd get lost in your Merage of friends."

"Are you serious?" I ask.

"Come on, Xander. You had around 4000 friends at the time. I was just one of many profiles."

"No, you were more than that," I respond, kissing her forehead.

"Ok, I know your first message was something you probably send to everyone, right?" Charlie asks, and I nod. "What made you continue the conversation?"

"What made me continue the conversation? Well, I enjoyed talking to you for one. Then I realized pretty quickly that there was something about you I craved. How about you? Why did you respond or continue talking to me?"

"The truth is, I wanted to be polite. If I didn't answer, it would have been rude. Once we started really talking, I knew you were someone I didn't want to lose."

"Any regrets?"

"None whatsoever. I can say that with certainty," she replies, and I smile.

"None here either."

Once we get back to the house, I watch her pull her hair up into a ponytail, and she turns to look at me.

"What?" she giggles.

"I am going to go into my office to get changed. It will take ten minutes. I want you to go into my bedroom and change into the bra and panty set I have laid out on the bed. While in there, take a look at what I have displayed on the dresser; these are the tools I may use on you. When I come into the room, I expect to find you kneeling on the floor, waiting for me," I instruct, kissing her cheek before walking into my office.

Chapter 34

Charlie

I close my eyes and take a deep breath. My heart is pounding, and I notice my hands have become shaky. My life is about to take a path I would have never imagined, not even in my wildest of dreams. I would lie if I said I wasn't nervous. I am so anxious but excited at the same time. To be honest, it's a feeling I want to remember for the rest of my life. It reminds me of the fight or flight response you get when faced with something difficult. I have either option at this point, and knowing the person I used to be, my first choice would be to flee. That's not the woman who is here today. Today I will fight, push myself to the edge, and break boundaries. He's prepared me for this, given me the tools to discover who I really am and who I want to be. I trust him, and I know he will keep me safe. Suddenly, I hear footsteps approaching. Opening my eyes, there he is, looking down at me, glaring directly into my soul and I immediately feel calm. My eyes move up, looking at his hands. A small grin graces my lips when I see what he is holding.

"Shall we?" Xander asks.

"I'm ready," I reply.

He unlatches the black leather collar and places it around my neck, fastening it with a lock, placing the key on his dresser. He walks back over to me, hooking the leash on the silver clasp in the front.

"Welcome to consideration time," he says, pulling the leash, making me stand up.

The moment I feel that jerk, a rush shoots through me, and my heart starts to beat fast again. I am standing in the middle of his bedroom, wearing a lacy black bra and panty set with a collar and leash around my neck, Xander staring directly into my eyes. For a moment, I feel helpless, unsure what to do, but then I remember, I am not in charge, I wait for his command, and a part of me feels relief. God, the sight of him in his dress pants and white button-down is incredibly sexy, how will I contain myself not to fall all over him?

"Come," he says, pulling the leash and leading me over to a large standing mirror.

Placing me in front of it, I take a look at my reflection, and I don't see an ounce of fear in my eyes, just pure lust, and anticipation. The feeling of the collar around my neck is...unexplainable, but in a way, it feels as if it's always belonged there. It's in the mirror that I notice the initials X and C, he's thought of everything.

"Are you ok?" Xander asks, running his finger over the rim of the collar.

"Yes," I reply, and before I can say another word, Xander pulls out a blindfold and places it over my eyes. As I hear the click of his belt buckle, I feel myself being pulled down with the leash until I am forced to kneel.

"All fours and open your mouth," he demands, his tone authoritative. Immediately he shoves his erect cock past my lips, groaning instantaneously, turning me on to the point that I feel myself become even more aroused. I don't know if it's because I'm blindfolded, but his thrusts seem very different from before. A bit rougher, almost like he is challenging me. To be honest, I'm not sure if I really like this, but I'm not giving up yet. He has a tight grip on the leash, so even if I would try to move back, I'm not sure I would get very far. Feeling him shift slightly, his free hand runs down my back and over my ass. Suddenly, I feel his fingers slip into my panties and deep inside of me, almost mimicking his cock deep in my throat. Moving them in and out, his hand seems to be getting caught up in the material of the panties, so he lets out his displeasure with a loud groan before literally ripping them off me. Surprised, I gasp, but with his cock in my mouth, it only ends up making me gag. I feel him let up on the leash a bit, slowly pulling his cock out. I can feel the saliva run out of my mouth and onto my chin, so I attempt to turn my head to wipe it away.

"Do not move," he demands, and I freeze.

"Sorry, I was trying to wipe the saliva from my mouth," I reply, still completely still.

"I know. That's why I stopped you. I love seeing you this way. Stay perfectly still."

I'm feeling slightly awkward, to tell the truth. On the floor on all fours, saliva still running out of my mouth, torn panties hanging on my right thigh, blindfolded, and knowing fully well that Xander is standing there just staring at me. I take a deep breath and try to think of something else; I don't want him to feel my insecurity right now. Moments later, he releases the leash and walks away. Not even twenty seconds later, I feel him approach, and I wonder what's about to happen next. From what I can tell, he is walking circles around me, completely silent. Out of nowhere, I feel something run up my back, and I jerk.

"Be still. Last warning," Xander threatens, and I'm not sure how the hell I am supposed to hold still when he is doing this to me.

His hand makes its way to the back clasp of my bra, undoing it and slipping it off my shoulders, letting it fall to the ground in front of me.

"Up on your knees. Right arm, hold it out," Xander orders, and I do as I am told, my bra still hanging on one wrist.

Xander removes it, and his hand grabs mine. He kisses the palm up to my wrist, and a small smile comes over my lips. Holding my hand, so my arm stays stretched out, he runs whatever he used on my back up my arm, and I exercise all of my self-control, so I won't move. From the feel of it, I realize it's the crop, and excitement shoots through me.

"Good girl," he comments, making my smile grow.

He continues running it over parts of my body, very slowly, and even though I can't see, I know his eyes are studying me. Grabbing the leash that has fallen between my breasts, he runs the crop over my right breast, down my ribcage, past my belly button until he reaches my vagina.

"Are you wet?" he asks, his breath on my ear.

"Yes," I reply.

"How wet?"

"Dripping."

"Exactly how I want you," he says, running the crop back up the front of me, releasing my hand.

Pulling the leash up to where I am standing, I feel what's left of my panties fall onto the floor and right then, a stinging pain on the left side of my ass.

"That's for moving," he explains, and by his tone, I know he is smiling.

"I apologize," I reply, a coy smile on my face. Fuck, what a turn on.

With the leash still in his hand, he leads me over to the direction of the bed... I think.

"Sit on the edge," he whispers into my ear, sending tingles through me.

My hands reach in front of me, trying to feel my way. His hand guides me, and I feel the soft sheet on the mattress. Turning around, my hands rest on the side of me, and I sit on the edge, wondering what is about to happen.

"Spread your legs," Xander says. "Wide."

I'm going to have trouble with this one. That is total exposure for sure, and I am blindfolded, missing an important sense. Then on second thought, maybe it's good that way. I begin to spread my legs, and I know they aren't as wide as he wants them. His hands grip my knees, spreading me open as far as he can, and his mouth finds my clit, sucking hard. Clutching the sheet beside me tightly, I begin to scream in pleasure, and his tongue moves up and down my vagina, driving me insane. With his hands still on my knees, I can feel nails digging into my skin. Throwing my head back, my moans fill the room, and his groans send vibrations through my body. I feel myself get close to coming, and he knows it, removing his mouth instantly, leaving me breathless.

Next, I feel his hands behind my head, removing the blindfold, and even though the room is dim, it takes a moment for my eyes to adjust. Finding his eyes, I stare into them, and what I see is a mixture of lust, longing, passion and a predatory look. The last is new to me, something I've never seen before, but I'm not afraid. This is the moment I also realize I haven't changed my position. Even though he removed his hands from my knees, I'm still sitting there, spread for him.

"You're so beautiful," Xander smiles, running his hand down my cheek. "Get all the way on the bed and lie back."

Once I lay my head onto the soft pillow, he joins me, lying next to me. Neither of us says a word, and I know I can hear his heartbeat. A slow rhythmic beat, very calm, and the opposite of mine. Well, what did I expect? He's been doing this for a very long time. A part of me wonders if it's still exciting to him or if it's just a habit or routine. Charlie, stop thinking, enjoy the moment. Xander places his hand on my cheek and leans in to kiss me, a beautiful, slow, lingering kiss. My hands make their way to his shirt, unbuttoning it, waiting for him to stop me, but he doesn't. Our kiss continues, and so do my hands, until I tear the shirt off him. He inches closer, his skin on mine, and now I'm determined to get those pants off. I want him now, I feel myself aching, needing him. To my surprise, he helps me, throwing his pants on the floor, but what comes next, I did not expect. He gets up, and I'm left lying on the bed, screaming inside, needing him to give me release. He walks over to the dresser and returns with a flogger. I can't help but smile. It's the tool I loved to play around with when he showed me his collection, the one I playfully used on him. The sight of him, naked, holding the flogger, sends goosebumps to my skin. Being blindfolded took away a major sense, and I had no idea what was coming next. Seeing what he is about to use is calming but exhilarating at the same time. Climbing back on the bed, he straddles me, running the flogger over my breasts, very slowly, traveling down my ribcage and back up to my breasts. I close my eyes, my hand gripping the pillow,

266

and I feel a slight whack on my right breast, opening my eyes.

"Eyes open Charlie, I want you to look at me. I want to see the longing in your eyes," Xander explains, and I nod.

He continues running the flogger up and down my body, at times reaching behind, stroking my legs all the way down, and back up. In a way, I want to close my eyes again, just to feel that warning once more, I loved it. I don't want to defy him purposely though, I can be obedient, and I will.

"Good girl," he whispers, leaning forward, close to my ear. "I think you deserve to be rewarded."

"Please," I barely make out, and then I feel his cock at my entrance, toying with me, rubbing the pierced head all along my sex lips. Fuck, he is such a tease. Once he finally enters me, he does it slow, not at all how I expected. Letting out a loud groan, he begins to thrust, deep, and I grip onto his arms, moaning, my nails digging deep into his skin. He lets out a carnal groan in response, his mouth moving to my neck and biting hard. I scream, and he picks up the pace, giving me my reward, two orgasms, back to back.

He withdraws immediately, and I slowly regain my composure as I see him reach into the drawer of the nightstand, pulling out a wand. Smiling, he raises an eyebrow and turns it on. That sound instantly sends tingles straight to my groin since I'm quite familiar with the wand. His hand travels to my clit, exposing it, placing the vibrating wand on it with more pressure than I would. I start to scream again, fuck this is intense, but Xander doesn't let up; instead, he begins fingering me at the same time. At this point, my eyes are closed, and I think he recognizes that the degree of pleasure he's giving me is bordering on torture. His hand continues to move inside of me as he keeps the wand in position. At this point, I actually can't tell what is making me come, his hand, the wand, a combination? I feel my legs begin to shake, as does my entire body. I've lost count of orgasms, but I know he is keeping track. The buzzing stops, but his fingers continue. I open my eyes, and he places the wand next to me on the bed.

"I want you now!" he demands, flipping me over, grabbing my arms and pulling me up to his chest. Kneeling, he releases my hands and tells me to hold on to the headboard. Spreading my legs with his, he grabs his cock, running it up and down my vagina, coating himself. He thrusts into me, and I throw my head back in response. His left hand travels to my breast, squeezing it tight as his right covers my neck, pulling me back toward his mouth.

"You are mine," he whispers.

"I'm yours, Sir," I reply, panting. "Entirely"

Did you enjoy the story? Check out other books by Drew A. Lennox

Feather – Book 2

Struggle – Book 3

Bound but not Restricted

The Twelve Days of Christmas Daddy Dom Style

Not your average Dom

Affliction

Printed in Great Britain
by Amazon

55879019R00155